The Director *of*
MINOR
TRAGEDIES

". . . a barren man in a barren land . . ."
—J. Hillis Miller

"All beginnings require that you unlock a new door."
—Rabbi Nachman of Breslov

"Let everything happen to you: beauty and
terror. Only press on: no feeling is final."
—Rilke

The Director *of* MINOR TRAGEDIES

Ronald W. Pies

iUniverse LLC
Bloomington

THE DIRECTOR OF MINOR TRAGEDIES

iUniverse books may be ordered through booksellers or by contacting:

iUniverse LLC
1663 Liberty Drive
Bloomington, IN 47403
www.iuniverse.com
1-800-Authors (1-800-288-4677)

ISBN: 978-1-4917-3193-2 (sc)
ISBN: 978-1-4917-3194-9 (e)

Printed in the United States of America.

iUniverse rev. date: 04/21/2014

He (RYB"Z) said to them (his five students): Go out and see which is a good path for a person to attach himself to. Rebbi Eliezer said "Ayin Tovah" (a good eye). Rebbi Yehoshua said "Chaver Tov" (a good friend). Rebbi Yossi said "Shachen Tov" (a good neighbor). Rebbi Shimon said "One who foresees the outcome (of his actions)." Rebbi Elazar said "Lev tov" (a good heart). He (RYB"Z) said: I "see" (prefer) the words (the opinion) of Rebbi Elazar ben Arach, for included in his words are your words.

Dedication

To Nancy, who makes it all worthwhile

Chapter 1

The One-Hit Wonder

Adam Levtov wondered if he had died in his sleep. Joel was texting one of his high school friends, oblivious to Levtov's synthetically cheery, "Hey, good morning, Dude!" Rebecca was on the phone with the roofing people, haggling over the estimate, which seemed to be coming in much higher than his lawyer wife felt justified. She was letting the roofer know of her intense displeasure, and did not turn her face from the phone when her husband entered the study, carrying a steaming mug of coffee.

Levtov wondered if he might be nothing more than a ghost unable to accept his own ghostliness. Or perhaps his body was now inhabited by a *dybbuk*—a wandering soul or malevolent spirit. From his father's Hasidic folk tales, Levtov recalled that the entry of a *dybbuk* into a living person's body signified the person's secret sin—the sin having opened a door through which the evil spirit can enter. Only Pupik, the family's runt of a cat, seemed to take notice of Levtov, briefly rubbing her scrunched-up face against the leg of his pajamas. He smiled, reassured briefly of his own corporeality.

From upstairs, the sound of his father-in-law's muffled soliloquy reminded Levtov that the dress rehearsal of *Othello* was only two months away. Sometimes, the old man's brain seemed uncannily intact, given his condition. But the doctors had taught the family that this was how Alzheimer's—if it was Alzheimer's—often worked. The patient might be able to repeat flawlessly some poem he had memorized in grade school, or sing a Frank Sinatra tune from 1963, yet be unable to remember that he had eaten breakfast an hour ago. Something about "Ribot's Law"—the oldest memories were the most resistant; the newer ones, fleeting as dandelion fluff. And now the words, though indistinct, were unmistakable: the old man was reciting from Othello, in that grandiloquent baritone he had burnished over fifty years ago: *"Rude am I in speech, and little blest with the soft phrase of peace."*

Act 1, Scene 3. For reasons unclear, from cerebral depths unknown, Eliezer Kornbluth always seemed aware of the play his son-in-law was working on. And as a professor of English literature for over fifty years, the old man had plenty of advice to offer, his dementia notwithstanding.

Now the voice from upstairs was louder, more melodic, and definitely not Shakespearean. *"Oh, do you know the muffin man, the muffin man, the muffin man . . . ."* Then a huge, clattering boom shook the entire house, bringing down a poorly-hung Manet from the living room wall.

"Adam!" Rebecca's voice rang out, "Would you please check on Pop! I'm on the phone with the roofer."

Levtov was already running late. In another half hour, he would meet his nine o'clock class, then attend rehearsal at ten-thirty. Jabari Frazier, the kid playing Othello, had a raw and powerful presence, but lacked finesse and was having trouble with the Elizebethan cadences. Levtov wondered if there was some unspoken resentment on Frazier's part, whose sullen looks and mutterings were now a growing distraction.

"Yeah, OK, I've got it covered!" he called back to Rebecca. Last week, it was Pop sneaking out of the house at five in the morning, winding up at the Levine's, and feeding their dog the thick, porterhouse steak Rebecca had bought for Saturday's dinner. "Sundowning," Dr. Stolberg had called it—but lately, Elie's confusion and wandering seemed to start closer to sunrise.

Levtov started to bolt up the stairs, then heard a hair-raising, "*Mryeeowwww!*" as his foot crushed Pupik's scrawny tail. *Poor, pitiful, Pupik*: the runt of the litter, tormented by her first owner's sadistic seven-year-old—and now so traumatized, you never knew if she would purr in your arms or take a claws-out swipe at your face.

Levtov entered his father-in-law's bedroom: the usual clutter of stained underwear, empty tins of smoked whitefish, and carelessly tossed texts of Elizabethan drama lay partly buried by the huge, oaken book shelf that had been toppled over, probably as the old man was rummaging for some arcane volume.

"Jesus, Pop, are you OK? We felt the whole house shake and . . ."

"OK, OK, am I OK?" Elie Kornbluth replied, staring at the floor. He was still in his pajamas, the bottoms of which revealed a dark, spreading spot near the old man's crotch. "How should I be? I have no staff, no retinue! My students have deserted me . . . Oh, *how sharper than a serpent's tooth it is to have a thankless child!*"

"Pop, listen—I have to get going to the college. Let's get you back in bed, OK, then Rebecca will come up and get the room back to normal, and . . ."

Suddenly, the old man's expression brightened, his face shorn of twenty hard years. "So, *boychik*, are you still working on *Othello*? Or do they have you back doing the dog-work plays? Othello, you know, it's very demanding. Edmund Kean collapsed during his performance in 1833—Act 3, Scene, 3. Then there was . . ."

"Yeah, Pop," Levtov interrupted, "I'm doing Othello. They gave me the good stuff this time. No more *Timon of Athens!*"

"Glad to hear that," his father-in-law intoned, pulling up his pajama bottoms and struggling to organize his tangled thoughts. Placques and tangles in the brain—that's what the doctors had told the family. "They need to make use of your talents, Adam. After all, how many drama teachers write a successful Broadway play, even if you . . ."

"It was off Broadway, Pop. And that was a long time ago. I'm the one-hit wonder, remember?" Levtov carefully maneuvered the old man back into bed and seemed eager to change the subject.

The old man's face quickly darkened. His eyes narrowed, as if to see his son-in-law more clearly. "Ah, yes. Isn't that what the Englishman in your department calls you? What's his name—Summerfield? Summerstock? Well, Adam, it's a shame, with all your potential! Honestly, my dear, how long are you going to let your guilt over that one play deter you from . . ."

"Pop, I really need to get going," Levtov interjected tersely, feeling his face fill with blood. "I'll get Rebecca to come up in a minute."

Levtov lifted the empty book case off the floor, leaving tattered volumes of Shakespeare, Spencer, Marlowe and Chekhov strewn about. Even in his demented state, Eliezer Kornbluth still managed to get under his son-in-law's skin. Being reminded of Ivor Somerset—that womanizing twit!—was bad enough. But being reminded of "Lustig the Tummler"—his smash-hit play—was the last thing Adam Levtov needed.

Pupik padded into the bedroom and rubbed her face against his leg, purring happily, forgetful of the injury Levtov had inflicted just minutes ago. He patted the tiny creature on the head, then bounded downstairs and into the kitchen, where Rebecca was pouring herself a cup of coffee and Joel was munching on a bagel.

"Pop's OK, Bec," Levtov announced. "He knocked over the big book shelf, but he looks fine. Except he peed in his pajamas again. Can you handle it, hon? I have to be at the college in a half-hour and I'm still in my PJs."

Rebecca stirred some dry milk in her coffee, a deep furrow creasing her brow. "Yeah, well, I'm supposed to meet with the partners in twenty-five minutes, and Marisol doesn't get here for another fifteen!" At seven-thirty in the morning, Rebecca Levtov was dressed in an impeccably tailored tweed suit, her auburn hair perfectly coiffed, her black leather attaché case at her side. At forty-three, she still looked like the fresh-faced co-ed Adam had met at Cornell, more than twenty years ago. But at the moment, her face was tight with worry.

"Well, Jesus, Bec, he's *your* father! I can't miss a class just because . . ."

"Dad, Mom, chill *out*!" Joel interjected loudly. His voice cracked as morsels of bagel fell from his mouth. "I can take care of Zayde until Marisol gets here. I don't have to be at school until, like, eight-twenty."

At fifteen-and-a half, Joel Levtov seemed suspended in hormonal limbo. Though he had sprouted a bit of dark "peach fuzz" on his upper lip, his sexual development had been slower than many boys his age. *He's a good boy,* Levtov thought, *but so hard to read.* Lately, Adam could barely look at his son without fixating on the streak of bleach-blond hair the boy had introduced a few months ago, not long after the gold earring had appeared. What could this mean—this platinum slash, amidst the boy's coal-black curls? Adolescent rebellion was one thing—but was there more going on? Levtov felt his gut tighten. There was that time he had walked into Joel's bedroom and found his son snuggled up close to his friend, Seth, who also favored an androgynous, quasi-Goth, "emo" look. But really—who knew, at age 15, what his erotic trajectory would be, especially in an era when sexual fluidity seemed so common? For that matter, who knew for sure, even at age thirty?

"Oh, that would be *suuuper*, Joel!" Rebecca chimed in, her face relaxing into gratitude. "Oh, and, Joel—sorry, but Zayde will probably need changing before Marisol comes."

Cacophony, chaos, coffee—and somehow, the morning would be gotten through. Levtov, in the space of twenty minutes, would down a cup of French-roast; eat a piece of whole-wheat toast, generously spread with blueberry jelly; shuck his pajamas; throw on his shirt, slacks, and patched, Harris tweed jacket; shove a pile of newly-graded papers into his briefcase; and drive three miles down the road to Hope Falls College, where he taught drama: the department's director of Shakespeare's minor tragedies. This diurnal ritual, repeated with only a few variations over the past twenty years, was far from the vision Levtov had nurtured as a young playwright, yearning for the fabled "bright lights of Broadway." And it was far from the life of rabbinical scholarship young Adam's father had begged his son to undertake. *And yet, and yet*—the ritual had its quiet blessings. And it would get Levtov through another morning.

*   *   *

Chapter 2

Old School Ties

Levtov had five minutes before his first class. He placed three scoops of French roast into the filter basket of the old "Mr. Coffee"—the same machine he had purchased in 1998, for $12.95. He was still an assistant professor then, on a piddling salary, but he had achieved the status of "rock star" in the department. The off-Broadway debut of "Lustig the Tummler" had left even the placid and scholarly department chair, Creighton Fitchley, in a state of buzzing befuddlement. No one in the history of the tiny department—not even Ivor "Golden Boy" Somerset—had ever achieved fame as a playwright. Above the coffee maker, Levtov had hung a memento of that shining moment: a black-and-white photograph, taken outside the Second Stage Theater on West 43d Street, showing the young Levtov holding a glass of champagne, as Rebecca—one arm around her husband's neck—blew a kiss to the photographer. Next to the photo was a framed review from the June 12, 1998, *New York Times*, proclaiming,

"A Lusty Lustig Comes to Town." Ben Brantley had been kind in his review, and—thank God—had not suspected the bit of literary larceny that had beclouded Levtov's life, ever since. Only two people besides Levtov himself were aware of his perfidy—and one of them was in the middle stages of dementia. "Lustig" had enjoyed a brief revival at Second Stage, in 2012, but closed after only a week. Whether the failure was due to the new and much younger cast; the more cynical critics; or the less forgiving, "gotcha" culture of post-9/11 America, Levtov couldn't say—but after the play folded, the name "Lustig" never came up again in the Levtov household. Nothing was said in the department either, except for Ivor Somerset's unctuous, "Bad luck, old boy, bad luck!"

Back in the play's glory days, Levtov had imagined that his newfound fame might advance his status in the department—yet if anything, the opposite had occurred. With only five faculty members in the entire department, it did not take long before the initial congratulatory back-slaps gave way to looks of sullen envy and resentment. Somerset— whose glamorous good looks called to mind the young Peter O'Toole, dashing around the sands of Arabia—took it harder than the others, gilding his acrimony in fulsome praise.

"Well, well, well, dear boy!" Somerset would greet Levtov, clapping his hand upon the young playwright's shoulder, "How is our budding, off-Broadway bard? Bearing up under the blandishments of the paparazzi, are we?" Somerset had the habit of bringing his chiseled, Saxon face uncomfortably close to Levtov's, often exuding a boozy familiarity that Levtov found both obnoxious and oddly unsettling. Somerset also exhibited that insidious, Oxbridge form of anti-Semitism that was nearly impossible to spot, unless you were a member of "the Tribe."

"Now who would have thought," Somerset would go on, "that a play about a little, Jewish clown would wind up a great, stonking hit!"

"A 'tummler' is not a clown, Ivor." Levtov would remonstrate. "A tummler is, well . . . somebody who makes things happen. He's a combination of comedian, activities director, MC . . ."

"Yes, yes, of course, dear boy, we are all well informed in the matter of quaint Yiddishisms, your people having been fruitful and multiplying in such great numbers. Oh, by the by, I meant to ask you—how *is* your charming wife doing these days? Olivia and I would love to do dinner again sometime . . ."

Ever since Somerset's early years in the department— he had preceded Levtov by three years, having arrived from Cambridge, in 1992—the Englishman had made little secret of his attraction to Rebecca Levtov. Nominally, Somerset was married to Olivia—a slender, attractive woman in her early 30s who had the odd habit of clearing her throat after nearly every sentence—but this inconvenience barely slowed Somerset's prodigious womanizing. And, owing to his cinematic good looks and sinuous charisma, Somerset was widely seen as the drama department's "leading man"—in terms of both directing the major productions, and even, at times, of taking on a cameo role in the plays themselves.

In contrast, over the past fifteen years, Levtov had been given responsibility for what the department chair tactfully referred to as, "Shakespeare's less appreciated works." In practice, this meant putting together a yearly production of either *Coriolanus* or *Timon of Athens,* each of which held the same degree of interest for Levtov's students as a Saturday night spent mopping the residence hall lobby.

"Ah, but Adam," Creighton Fitchley would remind Levtov periodically, *"Coriolanus* has so many modern, political overtones! Power, pride, the politician with the tragic flaw . . ." Fitchley—a slender, compact man with horn rim glasses, thinning gray hair and a wispy moustache—was a distinguished scholar of Elizabethan drama. He had been recruited from Harvard in the early 1960s—at considerable expense—to head the fledgling drama department at Hope Falls College.

And so, each year, Levtov would struggle to transform a small troupe of enthused but largely clueless theater arts majors—mostly kids who wouldn't know *Coriolanus* from Cory Booker—into competent speakers of Elizabethan English, from whose mouths emerged such noble lines as, *"Would you have me false to my nature? Rather say I play the man I am."* And each year, Levtov's production of Shakespeare's minor tragedies would be attended by the proud parents of the student actors; the drama department faculty and their bored spouses; a few surly profs from English and Comp Lit; and a tiny coterie of red-eyed, Hope Falls students who seemed under the influence of one or another substance of abuse.

But this year was different. This year, Levtov had pleaded with Fitchley to give him one of the Bard's major tragedies.

"I can do it, Creighton, just give me the chance!" Levtov had said, pacing around Fitchley's tiny, book-lined office.

"Hmm, yes, well, Adam—you know we normally hand over the big plays to Ivor. He has a way, a style . . ."

"Creighton, please, you don't need Ivor—I can do this!"

Levtov's first choice would have been *Macbeth*, but he offered no arguments when Fitchley, thoughtfully tapping his moustache, said, "Hmm, hmmm . . . well, alright, then—let's have you try *Othello*. The students should like that one."

And, indeed, Levtov thought: what's not to like? A play involving a noble, Moorish general (often played, nowadays, by African-Americans like James Earl Jones and Laurence Fishburne); an allegedly unfaithful wife; and a scheming, treacherous villain—the kids should love it! Levtov nearly cackled, leaving Fitchley's office. It was only over the subsequent week that Levtov became fully aware of the burden he had assumed, and its attendant pressure. With the question of his promotion coming up in a few months, a lot was riding on the success of this performance.

Of the twenty theater arts majors enrolled in his Elizabethan Drama 302 course, only six seemed to have real acting talent. Of the two African-American students in the course, Jabari Frazier would be the clear choice for the role of Othello. Levtov was not wedded to the idea of a black man playing Othello—after all, Laurence Olivier and, more recently, Patrick Stewart had played the role—but Jabari Frazier seemed the natural choice. Though quiet and a bit shy in class, Frazier—once you put him on stage—was alchemically transformed, radiating the "fiery openness" Samuel Johnson had so aptly ascribed to the character of Othello: a man Johnson read as ". . . magnanimous, artless, and credulous, boundless in his confidence, ardent in his affectation, inflexible in his resolution, and obdurate in his revenge.". And it didn't hurt that Frazier stood at about 6 feet 2 inches, with the chiseled physique of a gladiator.

The problem, Levtov knew, would be the young man's diction. His family hailed originally from Atlanta, Georgia, and had moved to Syracuse when Jabari was 16. Now, at age 20, the young man's speech was still sprinkled with metathasized forms like "*aks*" for "ask", and irregular perfect progressives like, "He been workin" for "He has been working." Yes, Levtov was familiar with the sociopolitical arguments in favor of preserving Frazier's natural speech— thus honoring what linguists call, "African American English." But Levtov simply could not abide such a jarring break with classic, Shakespearean diction.

Just as Levtov was filling his mug with the steaming, freshly-brewed French roast, he noticed an unopened letter in his "in" pile. Instantly, his stomach made a noise like the mourning doves that roosted in his yard. The envelope bore the same unmistakable foreign stamp and the same wild scrawl in the address. It was the second letter in two months from Grigory Ignatieff.

*   *   *

Chapter 3

Do You Want to Satisfy Your Wife Tonight?

Levtov awoke with his heart pounding and his pajama top soaked in sweat. He glanced at the glowing hands on his watch and groaned silently: *5:13 am*—too early to get up for work and too damn late to get back to sleep. Like so many dreams over the years involving his father, this latest nightmare was set in the old family house in Batavia, where Isaac Levtov had served as rabbi for the tiny Orthodox congregation of Temple Beth Shalom. In the dream, young Adam was sitting at the dinner table with his mother and father, eating smoked white-fish. Candles burned brightly in the large, silver candelabra, and a fragrant loaf of *challah* lay steaming on a Delft Blue dish. Adam was thirteen or fourteen; his father and mother, around forty. Adam had grown his hair out into a shaggy extravagance of dark curls, which Rabbi Levtov had found "slovenly and effeminate." Suddenly, young Adam was choking on a fish bone, clutching his throat and gasping for breath. He reached out to his father, who sat across from Adam, stony-faced and motionless. His mother appeared stricken by her son's predicament, but said nothing. Finally, as his son turned a ghastly gray, Rabbi Levtov intoned solemnly, wagging his finger, "This is *HaShem*'s punishment, Adam, for turning your back on your people and your family!"

Sitting up in bed, wiping his brow with a tissue, trying not to awaken his softly snoring wife, Levtov pondered the accusation. It was not without foundation. The betrayal had occurred on several levels, if you wanted to examine it across Adam Levtov's lifespan. There was, at the age of eight, the boy's stubborn refusal to go to Hebrew school—a rebellion quickly and decisively quashed by Adam's parents. At age thirteen, there was his refusal to become a "son of the commandment"—a *bar mitzvah*—followed by his sullen acquiescence in the rote motions of the ceremony. At eighteen, there was Adam's decision to attend Cornell, spurning his father's impassioned pleas to apply to "RIETS"—Yeshiva University's Rabbi Isaac Elchanan Theological Seminary.

"Cornell, Schmornell!" Rabbi Levtov had scoffed. "*Nu*, Adam, you want to waste your good, Jewish brains learning chemistry and physics?"

"Jesus, Dad," Adam had replied sullenly, "not physics! *Literature.* I want to study literature, and I actually don't care what you think about that." Upon hearing such disrespect, Rabbi Levtov had left the room without speaking a word.

But broadly construed, Adam Levtov's betrayal of the Jewish people might also include his literary deception—the one that had made his name, so many years ago. After all, doesn't Rabban Shimon, the son of Gamliel, teach us that, *"The world is preserved through three things: truth, justice, and peace . . ."*? What sort of truth is it when you steal from another writer and entomb the fraud in your heart, for fifteen years?

Carefully, so as not to wake Rebecca, Levtov wriggled on his belly and gradually lifted himself off the queen-size bed. He decided to head downstairs and turn on his laptop before Elie started yelling, before Joel was out of bed, before anyone was up, save for the slinking, night-prowling Pupik. In his study, just off the kitchen, Levtov's laptop was already registering the endless stream of useless email, most of which was either unfiltered spam or unwanted requests from "all the little sparrows", as Levtov would describe them to Rebecca: would Professor Levtov like to attend this or that conference (no expenses covered, of course)? Would he agree to review (with no remuneration) a paper for the *American Journal of Theater Arts*? Would he consent to speak at the Hope Falls Depression and Bipolar Support Group, on the benefits of drama therapy? (How about academic melodrama as the cause of depression? Levtov wondered). And today's special, the first email in the queue: *Do You Want to Satisfy Your Wife Tonight?*

Um, well, yes, that would be nice, Levtov mused, quickly deleting the ad for bootlegged, Colombian Viagra. Lately, he was not so sure how well he had been "satisfying" Rebecca, though she never complained about his so-so sexual prowess. At age 45, Levtov's nether tissues—strictly speaking, his *corpora cavernosa*—were literally less sanguine than when he was in his 20s, at the top of his sexual game. Then there was the matter of Rebecca's salary. Though there was no logic to it at all, his wife's six-figure salary somehow rankled. Set beside the paltry figure of $63,412—Adam's yearly salary from Hope Falls College—Rebecca's income left him feeling effete and depleted. Then, too, with her lawyer's work-load—often taking her well into the night, and requiring multiple phone calls to the partners—Rebecca was often too tired for anything more than a peck on the cheek from her dispirited husband.

And, now, there were the constant traumata of Elie's dementia and its attendant periods of what the doctors called "disinhibition"—Elie's singing loudly at 4 a.m.; throwing a book against the wall of his bedroom; shouting profanities at either Adam or Rebecca; and, more recently, wandering around the neighborhood and causing mayhem. Not a pattern, frankly, that conduces to Dionysian love-making. Of course, Elie had frequent periods of lucidity, during which the "old Elie"—the esteemed Yale professor—would emerge, as if from some primeval mist—but over the last year, these interludes had grown shorter and more scattered. The question of a nursing home had come up repeatedly, of course, but Rebecca was adamant: nobody was going to put Pop ". . . into one of those God-awful homes, with their snot-green walls and carpets stinking of pee!" Never mind that the premier nursing home in the area, just down the road in Cazenovia, looked more like the Ritz-Carlton than an institution for the infirm elderly.

And there were darker concerns—perhaps justified, or maybe the product, as he lay awake at night, of Levtov's lifelong insecurity. It had started with a bit of flirtation at the faculty dinner three months ago, when Ivor Somerset had placed his hand on Rebecca's knee, as the two sat on the couch, downing Manhattans and hors d'oeuvres. Rebecca's face had flushed, but she did nothing to discourage this carnal incursion until Levtov moved closer to the two of them and lamely interjected, "So, how about that garlic shrimp, you guys?" (Hand removed, but without a flicker of guilt on Somerset's movie star features; skirt tugged quickly down over the knees, but too late to ease Levtov's misgivings). Then there was the note Levtov had spotted one night last month, as Rebecca's attaché case lay open on her desk: a piece of Hope Falls College stationery, bearing an undated, hand-written message:

> *Love to see you again for dinner. No hanky-panky,*
> *but hanky per se is certainly permitted!—Cheers, Ives*

"Ives", as anyone in the Hope Falls drama department knew, was the nickname of Ivor Somerset. An innocent construction of the note might have supposed that the "dinner" in question was the same faculty function at which said Somerset had deftly palpated Rebecca's knee—and that the "hanky" business was just the Englishman's usual, puerile lasciviousness. A less benign interpretation—the one that kept Levtov ruminating at night—was that Somerset, the arrogant prick, was well and truly *shtupping* Rebecca.

Cuckoldry, as Levtov well knew, was a staple of Shakespeare's comedies, including *The Merry Wives of Windsor, Cymbeline,* and *Winter's Tale.* "Wearing the horns"—an allusion to the submissive habit of stags, who forfeit their mates when bested in combat by another male—was always good for a laugh, on stage. But was there really anything funny about a husband who, having discovered in his wife's briefcase an apparent love note from another man, simply let the whole matter drop—no muss, no fuss? Levtov wondered: could such a husband lay claim to possession of the all-important Y-chromosome? For that matter, could such a craven creature claim to be fully and truly alive?

*   *   *

Chapter 4

Why Plastic Surgeons Hate this Hope Falls Housewife!

Rebecca Levtov gazed in the mirror and sighed. In the dawn's surly light, the dreaded doubling was revealed. True: for a forty-three year old woman, she was considered very attractive—this, she understood. And it wasn't just Ivor Somerset who provided ample evidence of her comeliness: male heads would turn in the supermarket, on the sidewalk, and especially in the law office of Malamud, O'Brien, Freund and Levtov. Hungry male eyes—God, those salivating junior partners!—would track the slow sway of Rebecca's hips, and—how did James Joyce describe the fundamental anatomy?—that region "where a woman's back changes its name." Ah, but the chin, the *chin*—that drooping, duplicitous flesh!

The previous day, Rebecca had gone online to seek remedies, and the first website to appear produced one of those obnoxious pop-up ads that seemed to know where she lived and what she was worried about: *"Why Plastic Surgeons Hate this Hope Falls Housewife!"* Rebecca could not resist the tug of this faux-personalized *exposé* and promptly clicked on the ad, which revealed the shockingly simple solution:

> *There are several chin exercises that you can do if you wish to get rid of your double chin. For the first exercise, begin by opening your mouth wide. Next, move your lower jaw in a downward and outward direction as though you are trying to "scoop" something with your lower jaw.*

As she stood before the mirror, applying just a hint of eye shadow and a thin layer of Max Factor lip gloss, Rebecca Levtov began to take stock. What did Adam's father used to call it, in Hebrew? *Cheshbon ha-Nefesh?* An "accounting of the soul," though it always struck her as odd that "*cheshbon*" was also the Hebrew word for "check", as in, "Waiter, *cheshbon*, please!" She rubbed her lips together for even distribution of the gloss, chuckling at the brand name, "Max Factor"—the cosmetic brand Rebecca had used since her college days. "You know, of course," Adam's father had once intoned, "that the founder of the company was Maksymilian Faktorowicz, a Polish Jew." That was when Adam had first brought Rebecca home to meet his family in Batavia. A year or so later, Rabbi Isaac Levtov was dead of bone cancer.

So what was the state of Attorney Rebecca Levtov's soul these days? This was a tough nut to chew on so early in the morning, after only one cup of coffee, but Rebecca decided to do a spot-check of the old *nefesh*. Well, on the one hand, life was good on the level of mundane blessings, comforts and pleasures. Hope Falls was a lovely little town, if a bit on the Mayberryish side, what with everyone greeting one another—perfect strangers on the sidewalk!—with a cheery, "Hey, how's it goin'?" Adam was undeniably a good man, if also, on occasion, a bit of a mouse. A few drams more testicular fortitude was called for, Rebecca mused, when Ivor Somerset had his hand on her knee. Who's to say he wasn't contemplating a slow, crotchward crawl?—and poor, murine Adam had intervened with a question about garlic shrimp! Truth be told, Rebecca had been a little drunk and wanted to provoke just a scintilla of macho jealousy in her tweedy, diffident husband—apparently to no good effect.

Then there was their recent conflict over children, as in, "Do we want more?" Rebecca decidedly did not. Sure, Joel was a wonderful kid—good-hearted and reliable, even with his Emo-Goth rebellion and that ridiculous blond streak amidst his dark curls. (To be sure, there was some question as to where his sexual compass needle was pointing). But—*more* kids, at her age? Aside from the medical risks—miscarriage, maternal hypertension, Down's Syndrome—there were all the issues of taking care of another squirming, screaming creature. Why would a successful lawyer in her early forties want to return to the world of the "three B's"—burping, bathing, and bonding—when there were so many unsavored pleasures in the world? What about the art career she had longed for since college, but had failed to pursue? Oh, yes (Rebecca snorted at the thought)—and there was that fourth "B", butt-wiping. No: there would be no more gestating larvae, whatever Adam might wish.

And why was her husband so fixated on having another child, anyway? Wasn't this a bit, well—*womanish*? Or is this how the "New Age Guy" was supposed to think? Rebecca's rather cynical take on her husband's wish was that he secretly feared he had messed up with Joel, and now wanted another shot at fatherhood. "*He wants a do-over,*" was how she put the matter to herself, though never, of course, to Adam. Sure, her husband talked a good game about sexual freedom, fluid gender identities, and so on—after all, in the world of drama and stagecraft, "love is a many-gendered thing." But the fear that his son was gay, Rebecca felt, had to be weighing on Adam's mind. You can't be raised by an orthodox rabbi and not have at least a smidgen of guilt, stemming from that infamous "abomination" verse in Leviticus. Or maybe, Rebecca mused, Adam felt that another child would be his spiritual legacy, having disappointed his own father so bitterly.

In that regard, Rebecca, too, was bound to disappoint: her own father, even through the fog of Alzheimer's, continued periodically to ask, "So, Rivkaleh, when are you going to pop another one out of the oven?" Elie Kornbluth had never been an observant Jew, but had grown up in a Yiddish-speaking household in Brooklyn. Throughout Rebecca's childhood, he would call his daughter by the Yiddish diminutive of "Rivka"—the Hebrew equivalent of "Rebecca."

Adam and Rebecca had not been at loggerheads like this during the first few years of their marriage, a year or so after Joel was born. Rebecca was twenty-nine, and still climbing the ladder at what was then the law firm of Malamud, O'Brien, and Freund. It would have been a good time to conceive another little Levtov, but neither Joel nor Rebecca was ready for more child-rearing. Adam had just tasted the sweet fruit of success with "Lustig the Tummler," and was hungry for another hit. Rebecca knew that old Mr. Malamud—the firm's founder—was considering her, along with two male associates, as a potential equity partner in the firm. Although nobody said it out loud, it was well-known that few women embarking on motherhood had ever "made partner" at M, O & F, which had been a respected but quite conservative Syracuse institution for over fifty years. (Mr.

Malamud, now in his mid-eighties and in need of a cane, still came in to the office three times a week, though officially retired).

Then there was Pop—poor, dementing Daddy.

"Can you imagine me taking care of a newborn, while Pop is upstairs, throwing books against the wall?" Rebecca had shouted at Adam, during one of their recent tiffs. "Or while he's tearing around the neighborhood in his bathrobe, feeding our steaks to the Levine's golden retriever? Honey, give me a freakin' break!" Adam had offered no response, except to sink deeper into the plush cushions on their living room couch. He had seemed more subdued in recent weeks, ostensibly because of the pressures of directing *Othello*. But he had alluded vaguely to some "obnoxious letters" he had received over the past few months, without wishing to say more.

The idea of putting her father in a nursing home appalled Rebecca. Sure, the place in Cazenovia was nice enough, but—for god's sake!—this was the man who had raised her single-handedly after her mother died, when Rebecca was nine. This was the man who used to sing her Elizabethan lullabies when she was terrified of the bogeyman under her bed:

> *Balow, my Babe, lie still and sleep,*
> *It grieves me sore to hear thee weep.*
> *If thou be still I will be glad,*
> *Thy weeping makes thy father sad . . .*

Rebecca recalled the first time she had brought Adam home to meet the Great Man. It was the fall of 1989, when she was a sophomore, and Adam, a junior, at Cornell. Eliezer Kornbluth was then the Sterling Professor of the

Humanities and English at Yale, and widely regarded as the shining star of Shakespearean studies, this side of the Atlantic. But Kornbluth's scholarship extended well beyond the Elizabethans. He knew the Greco-Roman authors, from Sophocles to Livy. He knew the German playwrights, from Goethe to Günter Grass, and the Russians, too: Gogol, Chekhov, Andreyev, and Denisov. Adam, a comp lit major, was appropriately star-struck, having read Kornbluth's magnum opus, *Shakespeare and the Meaning of Mind,* from cover to cover. He and Rebecca had been dating—actually, as the euphemism has it, sleeping together—for about six months and had settled into the role of established couple. Though a bit guarded at first, and pedantically formal, the Great Man had served the two young people lemon tea and English muffins, all the while gently probing young Adam's trove of knowledge.

Rebecca, arranging her hair in the mirror, smiled at her recollection of the dialogue.

"So, tell me, Adam: do you favor a Freudian reading of Shakespeare or a Shakespearean reading of Freud?"

"Well, sir . . . I . . . uh . . ." a stunned Adam had stammered.

"Come, come, my dear, don't be shy! You're not being graded now . . ."

Elie Kornbluth had the somewhat grating habit of addressing anyone—male or female—as "my dear." His sentences emerged Athena-like, fully-formed and armed; and his ideas, crystalline, passionate, and final.

"You know, my dears, the Freudian map of the mind is quintessentially Shakespearean. The entire triadic structure of id, ego and superego is a kind of *mimesis* of the Bard's sonnets, you see. You know, of course, Adam, that the Shakespearean sonnet consists of three quatrains, in which the poet poses a problem—in essence, a quarrel among the three parts of the psyche—which is resolved in the final couplet. This is all quite analogous to the ego's mediation of id and superego. Indeed . . . ."

The recollection of her father's brilliant and ebullient self—his primal, passionate *nefesh*—now brought tears to Rebecca's eyes, smearing the carefully applied Max Factor volumizing mascara, which now dripped down to the traitorous, doubling chin.

*   *   *

Chapter 5

Weak or No Signal

Levtov had fifteen minutes before the morning's rehearsal of *Othello*: enough time to fire up old Mr. Coffee, check his email, and gather his notes for the day. He had walked down the corridor to his office with that familiar sensation of being invisible—or rather, *translucent*, like some flimsy, diaphanous gown. It was not so much that the secretaries and students ignored him, which might have been an intentional slight; it was more the sense that they were looking *through* him, with a kind of pitying knowledge of Levtov's nothingness.

His laptop was not connecting with the departmental server, and Levtov kept getting a message reading, "*Weak or no signal*." He decided to turn his attention to the unopened pile of "snail mail", which usually consisted of unwanted conference fliers, inconsequential memos from Creighton Fitchley, and the never-ending charity solicitations. At the bottom of the pile—still unopened—was the letter he had seen two weeks ago, bearing the postmark,

117630 MOCKBA / 16-10-2013

Suppressing a sudden loosening in his bowels, Levtov decided it was time to deal, once again, with Grigory

Ignatieff. He sighed deeply and tore open the envelope. The letter was written in Ignatieff's usual loopy, ornate penmanship, and phrased in the broken English of one who had spent just enough time in the U.S. to pick up the basics, along with a few incongruous tidbits of American slang:

My Dear Professor,

I hope weather in your city is as good as in my. Sunshine and birds singing. But here is question I worry lot about. Don't you see with own two eyes? Hypocrite I understand. I grow up in old Soviet Union. KGB, lying to save your ass, that's life. But stealing? Please share money from play, at least Levtov! Allow name of Ignatieff to be known in USA. Otherwise I find you and your family. I am old but strong. Speaking under truth, I keep handgun in cupboard. I hope this is not to scare you. Gun helps to me keep composure and peace of mind. Also, if no satisfaction, I hire throatcut lawyers.

Yours faithful,
Ignatieff

Levtov heard his bowels groan, and a sick queasiness nearly overcame him. *I am not what I am,* he thought, shaking his head. *I am not what I am!* He shoved the letter into his desk drawer and grabbed his briefcase, realizing that he was nearly late for the rehearsal. He locked up the office and tore down the hallway, which was strangely empty of students and faculty. Levtov suddenly wondered whether he was really in the corridor of Bradley Hall, which housed the Drama and Comp Lit departments, or still home in bed, dreaming of being in Bradley Hall. It had been this way in recent years: not simply the feeling that he was transparent, but that he no longer inhabited the physical world, the world of living, breathing flesh. What was that famous Chinese story—about the Taoist Master?

> *Chuang Tzu dreamt that he was a butterfly fluttering here and there. Suddenly, he awoke and found himself a man once again. But then he thought, "Was I before a man who dreamt about being a butterfly, or am I now a butterfly who dreams he is a man?"*

Suddenly, Levtov slammed into what could have been a brick wall, but was instead the six-foot-two inch, wall of muscle, Jabari Frazier.

"Yo, Professa Liftoff, I am *so* sorry, man! I didn't see . . . I was rushin' to get to the rehearsal on time, and . . ."

Jarred back to whatever reality this was, Levtov was close enough to Jabari Frazier to smell a soapy, lemony scent on his skin, imbued with a musky undertone. Levtov reared back, slightly dazed by the collision and pondering the dizzying effect of the young man's complex aroma. He resolved to say something, at some point, about Frazier's habitual "Liftoff" moniker.

"Oh, Jabari, hi! Sorry, it was my fault . . . I just wasn't looking where—anyway, you can't be late if the professor isn't there yet!"

The two of them walked briskly down two flights of stairs and entered the department's diminutive performance chamber—a space barely qualifying as an auditorium and smelling faintly of mildew and stale marijuana smoke. The other members of the cast had already assembled and were chatting nervously or manipulating their iPods. Levtov surveyed his young actors and inwardly sighed. *Behold, the fair Desdemona*, paragon of innocence and wifely duty— played by Brittany Kendrick, whose twin shoulder tattoos read, "Entry in Rear" and "Best in Show." Beside her was her lady in waiting, Emilia, played by the very zaftig Heather Schultz—known by her classmates as "Humpin' Heather," for reasons too obvious to belabor. Standing nearby, apparently closing some sort of deal on his cell phone, was Brabantio— father of Desdemona—played by Josh Altshuler, who had recently returned to campus after what was described as "a brief rehab stay." Only Iago, played by Shaun Brannah, seemed true to type. He was a compact, muscular kid from South Boston, whose left eye deviated outward and seemed to glow malevolently. When he spoke Iago's lines in Act 3, Scene 3, you believed them, even with the strong, Boston twang:

> *O, beware, my lord, of jealousy;*
> *It is the green-ey'd monster, which doth mock*
> *The meat it feeds on.*

In class, Brannah always seemed to be smirking at something and rarely spoke, though his essays suggested a quick and agile mind. *A fine Iago*, Levtov thought, tapping his chin and smiling. Someone who overturns Yahweh's, "I am what I am," and spews out, "I am *not* what I am!"

"OK, people!" Levtov shouted in his best impression of Coach Jurkowski, his junior high school gym teacher, "Let's get up on that stage and do this!"

The rehearsal was a mitigated disaster. Brittany Kendrick took Desdemona's lines and turned them into Valspeak, with those high-rising, terminal interrogatives linguists have called "uptalk":

Othello: Think on thy sins.

Desdemona: They are loves I *bear to you?* (with rising intonation).

As for Jabari Frazier, Levtov saw both promise and peril in the young man's performance. Physically, viscerally, no one could have embodied a more convincing incarnation of the Moorish general, boundless in confidence and obdurate in revenge. And—perhaps in contrast to the character's limitations—a fierce intelligence seemed to glow in the young man's eyes. But with Frazier's Southern speech patterns, Othello's lines too often emerged with words like "rebuke" sounding like "*ree*-buke," and "things," sounding like "*thangs.*"

Levtov suddenly felt a panicky dread welling up in his chest. He pictured the scene on opening night—just six weeks away!—with Creighton Fitchley shifting uncomfortably in his seat, and Ivor Somerset choking back howls of laughter. "Quite the bollocks you've made, old boy! Willy Mays playing Othello and . . . oh, yes, brilliant!—Whitey Bulger, as Iago!"

Toward the end of rehearsal, Levtov's cell phone went off, the cheery notes from Bach's second Brandenburg concerto startling Levtov and provoking peevish eye-rolls from the students. It was Marisol, calling urgently about Elie.

"Señor Adam, I am sorry to call you, but *Papi*—I mean, Señor Elie—he is on the loose again! The neighbor, Miss Levine, she call me, she want me to call *la policía*! I try calling your wife, but she is very busy in the law office . . ."

"OK, OK, Marisol, calm down and don't worry! I'll be there in ten minutes."

This is how it had gone for the past six months, with Elie: the former Sterling Professor of the Humanities and

English at Yale, now reduced to furtive wanderings and helpless incontinence. But this Alzheimer thing was more complicated, Levtov knew. Sometimes, for an hour or two, Elie Kornbluth was still the brilliant professor—the author of *Shakespeare and the Meaning of Mind,* which had won the National Book Award for general nonfiction, in 1987. At times, Elie would astound Adam with some piece of arcane wisdom or advice; and then, ten minutes later, the old man would be pissing in the kitchen sink, singing, *"Mein Shtetle Belz"* at the top of his lungs:

> *Belz, mayn shtetele Belz,*
> *Mayn heymele, vu ich hob*
> *Mayne kindershe yorn farbracht . . . !*

It was this "disinhibited" quality that had led one of the neurologists to suspect "FTD"—frontotemporal dementia—rather than Alzheimer's Disease. But FTD, the Levtovs were told, usually begins in the 50s or 60s, and Elie's problems didn't start until he was well past 70. The MRI had been "inconclusive," and Elie's neurologist, Dr. Stolberg, had been a little vague, too. "Sometimes what they have, you know, it's kind of a mishmash," Stolberg had told Adam and Rebecca, shrugging his shoulders a bit sheepishly. He had suggested an additional test called a PET scan, but Elie had adamantly refused. "I can assure you, Doctor," he had said to Stolberg, "I possess no pets, other than my familiar, Pupik the cat!" Unfortunately, the type of medication commonly used for Alzheimer's had not worked well for Elie. In fact, his outbursts seemed to worsen with it, and he was now taking only a small dose of an antidepressant called trazodone.

Belz, my little town of Belz
My home, where my childhood days passed . . .

Levtov sighed, recalling how Rebecca had wept when she heard her father howling out the Yiddish song from her childhood, as he filled the kitchen sink with his tea-colored urine.

*   *   *

Chapter 6

A Young Man Noble in Reason

Joel Levtov sat on his bed, guitar in hand, struggling with a
B flat minor chord and avoiding his algebra homework. *What
was the latest shit-head problem from Mr. Camieux?* (He, of the
polyester sports jackets, unfailingly speckled with dandruff).
"Find a number such that if 5 times the number is decreased
by 14, the result is twice the opposite of the number?" *Who
gives a flying frack?* Joel's best friend, Seth Greenberg, was
great with algebra, and Joel could text him later for some
help. Like Joel, Seth was into Emo-Goth clothes; black,
knee-high boots; and vampire movies. Seth habitually wore
a t-shirt that read, "I'm So Persecuted and Alone!!" which
never failed to crack Joel up. And, like Joel, Seth listened to
a lot of Bauhaus, and Siouxsie and the Banshees—music that
caused their parents psychological as well as aural pain. Two
years ago, Seth had introduced Joel to the U.K. band, The
Horrors, and their debut single, "Sheena is a Parasite," which
drove Adam and Rebecca nearly to the brink. But for all his
little rebellions, Seth planned to go into computer science and
could solve Mr. Camieux's algebra problems almost as quickly
as the old man could write them on the whiteboard.

The two boys often had animated arguments about the
difference between "Emo" and "Goth" culture, which were

usually resolved over a few joints, at Seth's house. Once, sitting on the bed in Joel's room, Seth had put his arm around Joel and seemed to be leaning in for a kiss. At that point, Joel excused himself and fled to the bathroom, his face flushed and his head pounding in excited confusion.

Joel and Seth were among five kids at Hope Falls High School who had adopted the "Goth" culture. The school had its dress code, of course, and you couldn't veer to the extreme without some repercussions. But the Goth kids repeatedly and gleefully tested the limits, with their wardrobe of deep reds, purples, and black; and those dark, long-sleeved shirts and high-collared coats.

Three months earlier, Joel had gone to school heavily made-up with black eyeliner, surreptitiously "borrowed" from his mother. Old Mr. Camieux, sputtering and fuming, promptly sent the miscreant boy to the principal's office, where Mr. Kasofsky made Joel wash off the dark, infernal stuff. "Who are you supposed to be, anyway?" the smirking Kasofsky had asked, "Cleopatra?" A call from Kasofsky to Rebecca Levtov—in the middle of her meeting with the law partners—led to a testy confrontation with Joel, later that night.

"Look, honey," Rebecca had said to Joel, in the sweet voice of reason, "you can wear whatever you want at home. Put on the ruffled collar, eyeliner, whatever. It's not that I'm against a little, um, creativity. But in school, there are certain rules, and . . ."

"Yeah, and who makes the rules, Mom? The kids don't have anything to say about the rules! It's all the freakin' Abercrombies who make them up."

"Abercrombies?" Adam asked, with cow-eyed perplexity, "What the hell is that, Joel?"

"Dad, it's like, Abercrombie & Fitch! A & F! Don't you guys read the papers? Their CEO just told the press that A & F only wants "cool kids" to buy their clothes. You know, like, Joe College, all-American-boy. I doubt they'd even let me into their freakin' store!" Joel's voice broke sharply on the last word, and Levtov felt his face redden. His own hormonal struggles of late-pubescence flashed in his mind: the humiliating crops of acne; the Neanderthal hair on his knuckles; and worst of all, the unruly urges he could neither suppress nor understand. Levtov resisted the impulse to comment on his son's overuse of the word, "like"—that epidemic verbal tic encoded in the genome of American teens—and spoke in his best, "sensitive dad" voice.

"So, um, Joel—all this Goth stuff, the eyeliner, the music, the vampire movies—is it about protesting conventional culture? A way to assert your own counter-values and . . ."

"Oh, Jeez, Dad, don't go all Dr. Phil on me! My friends and I . . . the way we dress, the music we play—it's . . . we just like this stuff, OK?"

Oddly enough, Joel's Gothic interests had brought him closer to his grandfather—closer, emotionally, than Adam—or even Rebecca—had ever gotten. For in addition to reading Edgar Allan Poe and Anne Rice's vampire novels, Joel and his friends also read a good deal of Shakespeare. The Bard's tragedies, such as "Romeo and Juliet," were a good fit with the "Romantic Goths"—a kind of subspecies within the Goth genus, whose members favored a soft, dream-laden literature. Some "RGs" even dressed in Elizabethan garb, complete with high, ruffled collars. Elie Kornbluth, it turned out, was much in sympathy with this counter-culture and was amused and entertained when Joel would come to chat—particularly when the boy would read to Elie from one of Shakespeare's plays.

"Oh, my dear!" Elie would chime in, his face illuminated with something like his old inner light, "you are very kind to regale me with Shakespeare! Very kind, indeed! Nowadays, everybody assumes I'm just a drooling fool. Now, I'll admit, my brain is a bit flummoxed, a bit addled—*"Who is it that can tell me who I am?"* as our good Lear asks—but I am still of a mind . . . a certain mind . . . Oh, Lord, what was I saying, my dear? I am a man of fragments now: pasted pieces of rage and dread. *"O let me not be mad, not mad, sweet heaven!"*

"Zayde, it's OK," Joel would reply softly, putting his hand on Elie's shoulder. "You don't have to remember everything. I *totally* like reading to you and talking to you! You treat me like, you know, a real person."

"And others do *not*, my dear? Why, who could not see in you a young man noble in reason, and infinite in faculties?" But Joel didn't grasp the compliment or its origins.

"Zayde," Joel said sullenly, "I don't think my mom and dad even wanted me. I mean, like, from the beginning. Dad has had this thing about me. I'm, like, this punishment that came down on his head, and I don't even know why! I mean, he was pissed off with me way before I got into all the Goth stuff."

"Ah, my dear—do not blame yourself! It's all the fault of that damnable play—that wretched "Tummler" production! Your father has never forgiven himself. Oh, *what will it profit a man if he gains the whole world and forfeits his soul*? Mark my words!

"Um . . . I'm not sure what you mean, Zayde, about my dad's play."

"Ah, these are foul whisperings, foul whisperings, my dear! I must say no more."

Joel had not pressed his grandfather on the matter of "Lustig the Tummler," nor had the boy confronted his father regarding the need to be forgiven. He wondered, instead, whether Zayde's brain was indeed addled; and his grandfather's allusion to the play, mere nonsense. And he wondered, as he had for most of his adolescent life, why his father seemed to shrivel beneath his skin whenever the two of them sat down to talk.

Now, compressing the strings of the first fret until his index finger hurt, Joel Levtov produced a resounding B flat minor chord, its sound nearly smothering the low groan that escaped the boy's throat.

*   *   *

Chapter 7

Early Bird Special

The flight from New York to Ft. Lauderdale was miserable, with heavy turbulence and wailing infants combining to leave Levtov in a state of queasy disgruntlement. He had a talk to present in Boca Raton, which meant an obligatory visit to his mother in Coconut Creek. Rebecca had stayed home, both to look after Joel and to deal with various crises at the law firm. And, truth be told, Rebecca had never been particularly fond of Adam's mother, who seemed a throwback to the days when wives were largely appurtenances of their all-important husbands. (It didn't help that, during a visit to Hope Falls many years ago, Adam's mother had commented unfavorably on Rebecca's prized recipe for stuffed cabbage).

Levtov's mood was not improved by the brain-smothering heat and humidity of southern Florida, even in early October. Exiting the airport terminal, the mephitic, diesel-fumed air hit him with the force of a blow to the head. Having been raised in western New York, with its knee-deep, cruelly enduring winters, Levtov found the Floridian climate enervating. And yet, he understood the appeal to so many of the retired elderly, who did not wish to end their days slipping on an icy sidewalk or collapsing in a snow-buried driveway in Buffalo. During the cab ride from the airport to

Windermere Meadows, Levtov reflected on his mother's long journey from Batavia to Coconut Creek; from rabbi's wife to solitary widow; and, very recently, from life-long student of Judaism to the more elevated status of Jewish educator, in her retirement community.

Esther Levtov, now 72, retained the compact and slender elegance her husband had so admired, when Adam was a boy. Though a denizen of southern Florida for more than twenty years, the rebbetzin—"The rabbi's wife," as she was still known—retained the dress and customs she had maintained for decades in Batavia, where she had played the role of "First Lady" in the tiny Jewish community. Having been raised in an Orthodox household in Brooklyn, Esther Levtov had found the transition to small-town life difficult, if not traumatic. Rabbi Isaac Levtov was a good man, but he was neither easy-going nor particularly affectionate. And, as a "pulpit rabbi" with many official duties, he relied on his wife to handle a multitude of social and educational functions. This was especially the case when one of the women in the congregation felt uncomfortable coming to the rabbi with a question, such as a matter relating to *niddah*—the laws and practices pertaining to a menstruating woman. Esther Levtov had only a few close friends in Batavia, and only one—Anna Milstein, a social worker by training—who could engage the rebbetzin in serious intellectual discussions.

Though not formally educated in rabbinics, Esther Levtov had earned a degree in Jewish Studies from Yeshiva University's Stern College for Women—having matriculated only seven years after the founding of the college, in 1954. She had always held onto the dream of earning her doctorate, but the duties of rebbetzin—not to mention those of motherhood—had worked unremittingly against her. In truth, Rabbi Levtov had never been keen on the doctorate idea, and had discouraged his wife in gentle but unmistakable ways. Adam could still recall his father's facetious and subversive "compliment" to his wife, over the dinner table: "Sweetheart, what do you need to become a doctor for? *Nu*, are you going to take people's pulses? Already, you are a wonderful teacher for the ladies in the congregation!"

Now, thirty years later, wearing a dark-blue, formal dress and a pearl necklace, her silver-gray hair arranged in a tight bun, Esther Levtov greeted her son with a fervent hug and a light peck on the cheek.

"Adam, darling! What, so *thin*? Rebecca doesn't feed you these days? How come she and Joel didn't fly down with you? Come, let me get you some chopped liver, I just picked it up today."

"Sounds great, Ma. You look wonderful! Life down here must be agreeing with you."

His mother shrugged, raised her eyebrows slightly, and asked rabbinically, "Should life agree with us? I don't know. But, these days, I mostly agree with life."

Indeed, Esther Levtov seemed relatively happy in the largely Jewish retirement community, notwithstanding her solitary state. She belonged to a small coterie of well-educated, mostly widowed, Jewish women who took advantage of the "Early Bird Specials" at the best kosher restaurants in Coconut Creek and Margate. She and her friends prided themselves on getting seated promptly at 3:30 p.m—and on their spirited discussions of religion, politics, and world events. In addition, for the past month, Esther had been teaching a small class for Windermere residents. "It's on a topic your father would have scoffed at," she confided to Adam, with a dismissive wave of her hand. "It's about the spiritual role of women in the Talmud. 'Too trendy!' your father would have said!" Adam thought he saw his mother's eyes tearing up slightly.

"Well, Dad scoffed at a lot of things, Ma, including almost anything I ever came up with."

Esther Levtov looked slightly uncomfortable. "Well, darling, your father wasn't such an easy man to get along with. But he loved you, Adam, for all his criticism and kvetching. Now, come and sit!"

They noshed on his mother's homemade *chalah*, spread with chopped liver and onions, and Adam poured them both some Pinot Grigio. His mother rarely partook of alcohol, but she kept a bottle of white wine on hand for friends and visitors. Adam, on the other hand, had little difficulty downing two or three glasses of wine at a single sitting. For an hour and a half, they ate and schmoozed. Adam told his mother of his teaching activities, and of his big plans for staging *Othello*. She spoke of the concerts she had attended and the books she was reading, mainly in the area of Judaic studies. But as Adam was finishing his second glass of wine, the pleasant buzz of small talk gave way to the dull pain of lingering resentment. He felt anger rising in his throat, and at last, guiltily gave vent to it.

"I have to ask you, Ma—and please don't take this the wrong way—I could never figure out why you didn't defend me, when I was a kid. I mean, when Dad would lash into me."

His mother took a sip of wine and smoothed her dress, as if to prepare for a speech. Her face grew slightly pale. "Adam, you know, it wasn't so easy being the rebbetzin. I always felt I had to—not obey, exactly—but, well, show *deference* to your father. *Nu*, darling, you know the term, *shalom bayit*?

"Yeah, sure. 'Domestic tranquility,' right?"

"Well, you are quoting the definition from Hebrew school! But it's more than that, Adam. *Shalom bayit*—it means, sometimes, you have to make concessions, compromises, even when you don't like it. And you were a handful, darling, I think you'll admit! Sometimes, it seemed like you were deliberately trying to get under your father's skin. Like that time, in junior high school, with the math exam! *Oy*, remember how the principal sent you home, and Dad . . ."

"Yeah, yeah—I remember," Adam said, irritably gulping down some more Pinot. "I cheated on the exam, right in front of the teacher. Looked right at Heshy Salzman's answer sheet, with Mr. McNabb standing right over me. Pretty stupid, huh?"

"But you were a very smart boy, Adam. So it must have been something else that—it was almost like you *wanted* to get caught! So, naturally, your father was furious. And humiliated! For him, it was, you know, *"a shandeh un a charpeh."* A shame and . . ."

"Yeah, I remember my Yiddish, Ma. A shame and a disgrace."

At this, Esther Levtov heaved a sigh that seemed to expel a tiny portion of her soul.

"You know, darling, I always wanted to have more children, and not just because they are a blessing and a mitzvah. I always hoped—this may sound funny—that maybe if you had a brother or a sister, things would be easier on you. I mean, that your father would have had . . . well . . ."

"More targets to shoot at?" Adam snickered and poured himself some more wine.

His mother laughed forlornly. "Well, that's one way of putting it! But, you know, after you were born, the doctors told me, that was it. I had a C-section, you know, and the doctor said I had a very weak spot in my uterus—it could rupture, he said, so no more kids." She sighed again and heaved her shoulders. "Well, as they say, that's water under the bridge."

"I'd like another kid, to tell you the truth, Ma. But Bec—Rebecca, you know, she just doesn't seem to want one."

"Well, I suppose I can understand—I mean, Rebecca is no spring chicken. But still—if she's able to have more kids, I don't understand why she would deny you such a blessing. Maybe you should see someone? A counselor, or . . . ?"

"Well, it's complicated, Ma. She has her job to think of, and then, of course, there's her father. Elie is getting harder and harder to manage, you know." Adam looked down at his watch. "Anyway, listen, I need to get to my hotel and polish up my talk for tomorrow. I really should get going, Ma."

His mother's face fell. "So soon? You just got here! I didn't even hear anything about Joel! Also, darling, I need to tell you about something. Actually, I have a few things I need to show you."

Adam was taken aback. "Oh? What sort of things?"

"Well, it's a long story. But, the other day, I was going through the shoe boxes in my closet—stuff I haven't looked at in more than 20 years, since I moved here. Well, one of the boxes had a pile of old letters in it—mostly just letters I had read and stuffed back in the envelopes, but—well, one of them was . . ." His mother paused, searching her son's face for a reaction.

"What, Ma? What's the big deal?"

"Well, it was an unopened envelope, very carefully taped up, and addressed to you—in your father's handwriting, which I would know anywhere. Of course, I haven't opened it. The envelope had a date on it from just before Dad died—but this is the first I've ever seen it. I'll get it for you, if you just wait a minute. Oh, and—one other weird thing I meant to tell you about. I received a letter in the regular mail, addressed to you, but care of my name and address. But the strange thing is, darling, the postmark was from *Russia*, of all places! And the writing—it was in this crazy scrawl that I could barely read."

* * *

Chapter 8

A Friend is a Second Self

Levtov did not open the letter from his father. The whole idea of confronting the dying words of the man whose faith he had betrayed—at least in his father's eyes—was more than Adam Levtov could deal with at the moment. After all, the play was to have its dress rehearsal in under a month. His father-in-law's behavior was becoming increasingly erratic, if not dangerous. Joel was growing more and more distant from Adam and Rebecca. The tension between Adam and his wife was growing, as Adam's suspicions about his wife's involvement with Ivor Somerset festered. (Talk about "the green-ey'd monster"!—the irony had not escaped the director of Othello).

And now, there was the appearance of another letter from Ignatieff—this time, turning up at his mother's address. How had this crazy Russian managed to track down Esther Levtov? And what were his intentions? On the plane ride home, Levtov opened Ignatieff's letter, and found still more reason for concern:

My Dear Professor,

Perhaps now you worry why poor mama is getting letter meant for you! But you fail every time I send letter to Hope Falls college, getting back to me—where is respect in that? Where is professor's integrity? Not to answer me, this is *nyet kulturny*—you know meaning? Americans would say, "you are asshole!" (I spend one year doing visiting scholar, N.Y.U., 1987-88. Then I come again to U.S. as tourist in 2012, when I see STINKING, FUCKING FRAUD play, "Lustig the Tummler" at Second Stage Theater, West 43d Street).

Levtov—is this Russian name? Now is time for Ignatieff and Levtov to meet, get to know you, settle old accounts. Otherwise, mama will be not so happy when men come to visit in Cocopuffs Creek. You stole from Ignatieff, dear Professor. Now you must make back credit for me. You read Sartre, "The Flies"? Do not be man "in bad faith"! You must be *kulturny* and become AUTHENTIC man. Write me at Moscow address (57, Arkhitektora Vlasova St). Give good dates, and I fly United States to meet you. I do not use e-mail since FSB (our new name for beloved old KGB) inspect closely all the electronics.

Most respectful,
Grigory Ignatieff

Levtov put his head between his hands and rubbed his temples. A deep queasiness had settled in his stomach, and he fumbled around in the seat pocket in front of him, looking for the airsickness bag. He wasn't sure how seriously to take Ignatieff's threat, but the thought of Russian thugs showing up at his mother's door pitched his heart into some weird arrhythmia that left him lightheaded. He signaled the flight attendant and ordered a half-bottle of Pinot Grigio, which he chugged down in a few frantic gulps.

The problem was this: the third act of his 1998 smash-hit play, "Lustig the Tummler" had been stolen from Grigory Ignatieff's play, Комик—roughly translated, "The Comic" or "The Comedian." The construction, "had been stolen", it occurred to Levtov, sounded more than a bit Nixonian, as in "mistakes were made." It would be more accurate to say that Levtov well and truly stole Ignatieff's work, though the back story was somewhat more complicated.

In 1996, during a visit to his father-in-law's home in New Haven, Levtov had stumbled upon an English translation of Ignatieff's play. This, while browsing through Prof. Kornbluth's magnificent home library, which contained several dozen volumes of the modern Russian masters. Levtov immediately recognized Ignatieff's jaw-dropping genius, as well as the close kinship between "The Comic" and Levtov's own inchoate character of Shmuley Lustig—a comedian-cum-MC, at a big, 1960s Catskills resort. But Levtov's play had run into a roadblock in Act 3, when his muse seemed to desert him.

Suddenly, before his eyes, he saw his salvation! As Rebecca chatted with her father, downstairs in the kitchen, Levtov photocopied act 3 of the Russian's play. His hands trembled and his mouth went cottony dry with the fear of discovery—yet, inexplicably, Levtov was filled with a kind of randy exhilaration, as page after page flew from the copier. His temples throbbed and a thin, red haze clouded his vision. But as he stuffed the manuscript in his briefcase, Levtov found himself fighting off an intense feeling of nausea, terminated by a series of dry heaves.

Of course, he had not lifted the third act of Iganatieff's play outright. Rather, as playwrights often do, Levtov had "adapted" the Russian's work to his own purposes, transforming Ignatieff's post-war comedy into the idiom of the Borsht Belt, circa 1962. The resulting production of "Lustig theTummler" in 1998 had been a resounding success. But the subsequent years of Levtov's life had been—with some notable exceptions—a rack of inquisitorial torment, punctuated not by the pop of snapping ligaments, but by the accusatory cries of his rabbinical conscience.

He sighed deeply as the big 757 banked and circled over New York. His presentation had gone reasonably well: the sort of humdrum talk that evokes polite smiles and sidelong glances from colleagues, which say to the speaker, "At least your lecture did not kill me, and now I get to have lunch!" The one bright spot in the Ft. Lauderdale trip—*actually, more of a penumbra,* Levtov now realized—had been his dinner with Gianni ("Johnny") Chalakian.

Levtov had first met his friend when Chalakian was a "pre-meddie" at Cornell, furiously pursuing the genetics of fruit flies and the pleasures of nubile coeds—the latter, clearly the higher priority. Chalakian was of mixed Armenian-Italian heritage, which gave him both a cosmopolitan palate and a tragicomic world-view. On the one hand, there was the world of Fellini and Puccini; on the other, the perpetrators of the Armenian genocide, invariably referred to as "the Turks, the fucking Turks!" Tall, broad-shouldered, and darkly good-looking, Johnny Chalakian, at age twenty, could hold his own in a discussion of Dante or Petrarch—*paesani,* on his mother's side—or hold forth authoritatively on neuronal transmission in *Aplysia californica*. Chalakian, whose exultant profanity was legendary on campus, radiated a pheromonal confidence that the young Adam Levtov had found both incomprehensible and irresistible. Problems that seemed insuperable or overwhelming to Levtov were like bonbons to Chalakian, who genuinely believed that life could be confronted and mastered, with sufficient will and energy. At the same time, the young pre-med student recognized that evil was a genuine presence in the world and would not be stopped unless faced down by people of courage and conviction. Chalakian and Levtov were almost inseparable during their college years and had maintained a close connection over the past two decades. Eventually, Chalakian ran through his bevy of coeds and got married, shortly after medical school. He and his wife, Jannie—a nurse practitioner—lived just outside Miami, and had raised three strapping, teenage boys. Chalakian was now Chief of Neurology at University of Miami Hospital and a professor in the medical school. He had made a special trip up to Ft. Lauderdale for dinner with his old friend.

The two men met in the lobby of *Ponte di Rialto*, known locally as the best Italian restaurant in Ft. Lauderdale. At forty-five, Chalakian had put on a few pounds and was sprouting some grey at the temples, but otherwise looked very much as he had during their college days. With mock solemnity, the two men greeted each other with the ancient, Roman handshake, in which each man grasps the other's right forearm—a ritual they had begun in their college days.

"You know, Levtov, we use that handshake in the hospital now, to avoid spreading the flu!" Chalakian said with a laugh.

"Yeah, but, do you remember the origins of it, Chalakian? It was to make sure the other Roman didn't have a dagger up his sleeve!"

"Fucking comp lit majors! Always with the classical allusions! So how the hell are you, Levtov? You look pretty fit for a sessile, middle-aged college professor!"

"Sessile? Hey, you have no idea how often I'm running away from my chairman!"

The two friends ate voraciously, divvying up the excellent chicken parmigiana, fettuccine alfredo and shrimp fra diavolo. A full bottle of *Nero D'Avola*—which Chalakian described as, "Sicily in a bottle," and, "a tribute to my Sicilian mother"—went down very easily. Within an hour, both men were, as Chalakian put it, *alticcio*—a little tipsy—and more loquacious and profane than usual, even by Chalakian's standards. Levtov had intended to get some neurological advice about Elie's condition, but the topic never came up. Instead, the two compared wives (both men concluded they had "married up"); commiserated about being forty-five (the occasional nocturia had already started for both men); and, of course, reminisced about their college days.

"You remember that dickwad, Howie Herskowitz?" Chalakian asked gleefully. "And what we did to that prick?"

Well, of course! How could Levtov forget? Herskowitz—another premed student, in Chalakian's genetics course—was what Jews would call a *macher*: very roughly translated, a pushy manipulator. Said Herskowitz, a ruthless competitor, had sabotaged Chalakian's fruit-fly experiment—the well-known "dihybrid cross" study, using *Drosophila melanogaster*—by spraying the adult-stage flies with insecticide.

"*Poof!*" Chalakian fulminated, "A month's worth of—literally—fucking fruit flies, dead at the bottom of those twelve glass vials! That maniac, Herskowitz—no better than the fucking Turks!"

"Yeah, the kind of guy who gives the Jews a bad name. Ah, but revenge was sweet—literally!"

The two friends cackled loudly, recalling how they had induced an unsuspecting Herskowitz to gorge himself on hash brownies, three hours before the final genetics exam. In the middle of the exam, the thoroughly stoned malefactor calmly arose from his chair, announced to the entire room that he was "fucking starving!" and gleefully marched off to College Town for take-out Chinese.

The long, indulgent evening had been pleasant. But gradually, almost imperceptibly, Levtov began to experience a peculiar sensation—something Chalakian would have termed, "autoscopic depersonalization." He felt as if he were floating outside his body, looking down at Chalakian and Levotv eating Italian food and schmoozing. Maybe he had imbibed too much *Nero D'Avola?* No, he realized, the feeling was more that of a dream state than of intoxication. It reminded him of a nightmare he still recalled from childhood, in which a five- or six-year old Adam was sitting at a picnic table with his mother and father. Suddenly, both his parents began to take on the features of bears—specifically, large, American brown bears. A psychic representation of the song, "The Teddy Bears' Picnic"? The young Levtov had always found the lyrics of that song a little creepy: *"If you go down in the woods today you better not go alone!"* In the dream, young Adam began to float above the picnic table, as his bear-parents stared straight ahead, as if unaware of what was happening. He had awakened covered in a cold sweat, crying for his mother.

At this surreal point in the dinner with Chalakian, Levtov realized that his face was flushed with shame. The shame was fueling his anxiety, and, he reasoned, causing him to feel as if he were floating outside his body. "Hey, Adam, you OK? You're sweating like a friggin' pig!" he could hear Chalakian saying in a muffled voice. "Too much 'Sicily in a bottle' for the nice Jewish, boy?" *"Nu,* why shame, darling?" Levtov could hear his mother asking.

Only later, on the flight home, did he begin to frame a possible answer. For many weeks, perhaps foolishly, Levtov had hoped to tell Gianni Chalakian about the letters from Ignatieff—and about the fraud he, Professor Adam Levtov, had perpetrated on the world of dramaturgy. He had hoped to tell Chalakian about the troubles he and Rebecca were having—and how Ivor Somerset might be *shtupping* Rebecca to a fare-thee-well. He had hoped to confess to Chalakian his shame over the son he had brought forth—the son who wore eye-shadow and girly clothing and appeared partial to boys. He had hoped for absolution from Chalakian, for this very shame, which he knew was a desecration of the love he ought to feel for his son. And he had hoped to ask his friend, the neurologist, about the sensation of translucent insubstantiality he felt, walking down the corridors of Hope Falls College: was there a neurological syndrome that described this phenomenon?

But Levtov had voiced none of this. Instead, he had gazed upon his friend's tanned and fleshy substance—upon the neurologist's golden life and glittering accomplishments—and realized that Johnny Chalakian would understand nothing of what Levtov felt.

Chapter 9

Brush Up Your Shakespeare

Jabari Frazier was in a foul mood. "Yo, Professa Liftoff!" he called out. "Man, ah jus' caint *do* this!" He threw his script on the floor and sat down at the edge of the stage, scowling. With less than a month to go, the play was looking like a train wreck. The main players knew their lines, but with their diverse accents and prosody, the production sounded like a colloquy at the U.N. cafeteria. In years past, of course, there had been minor problems with the students' diction and enunciation—but this year, the mélange of accents and dialects seemed especially incongruous. Brittany Kendrick was still doing her high-rising, Valspeak terminals. Shaun Brannah, trying to sound "British," was dropping his *r*'s in the manner of bad JFK impersonator *("And fuh Cassio, let me be his undah-taykah, you shall heah moah by midnight . . .")*. When Levtov tried to work with Brannah on his diction, the young man seemed to take it as criticism of his "Southie" accent. And as for Jabari Frazier—he seemed to be struggling with Levtov at every pass in the play's formidable linguistic mountain range.

Levtov had never subscribed to the view that American actors doing Shakespeare had to sound like Sir John Gielgud or Emma Thompson. Ivor Somerset—he of the plummy

Oxbridge accent—was dead set against American actors trying to sound British, even at the highest level of the American theater. "We do get a bit cheesed off when you Yanks try to sound like us," he had told Levtov once, "though your Gwenyth Paltrow isn't half bad." Indeed, Levtov himself had come under the influence of the great theater director, Sir Peter Hall, who believed that "accent" was less important than good breath control, when doing Shakespeare. Levtov had taken a master class with Hall, some years ago, and had learned the maestro's secret for doing proper Shakespeare: you breathe at the end of a line, never in the middle. And you respect the Bard's iambic pentameter. Accordingly, Levtov spent hours drumming "*de/DUM de/DUM de/DUM de/DUM de/DUM*" into his young actors' heads.

Jabari Frazier picked this up quickly, and delivered his lines with the proper metrical pauses and stresses. But the old, southern inflections seemed to devour his words, and—to Levtov's ear—made a line like

"My blood begins my safer guides to rule" sound more like,

"Mah bluhd big-*ee*ans mah sayfuh gahds to rule."

Levtov was at a loss. Every time he sat down with Frazier with the aim of "working on the diction," the young man grew tense and sullen.

"Jabari, please, I'm not trying to criticize you or be disrespectful. We all grow up with some kind of accent. Mine, for example—it's that terrible, western New York accent—mine tends to flatten out "a's", so that a word like "cat" sounds like *caaaat*. In fact . . ."

"Look, Professa," Jabari would interrupt testily, "I know you mean well. But, man, why you all up in my grill? I wanna do a good job, I really do. And this Othello—I *get* this dude! He's an outsider, you know what I'm sayin'? He doesn't fit in.

I get it! But you gotta understand, Professa Liftoff—all my life, what I heard from folks was, Jabari, you got to talk this way, you got to walk that way! And the way I speak, man— it's not just an *accent*! Where I grew up—the way black folks in Georgia talk—that's a *dialect*, you know what I'm sayin'? And it's got its own rules. It's not trash talk from some damn rapper on the street!"

Levtov knew he had deeply offended the young man, who, in so many ways, had captured the gravitas and nobility of the Moorish general. And yet, Levtov could not quite bring himself to accept Jabari Frazier—or to give in to him. He wondered if there was some part of himself that needed to struggle with the young man—or that resented him. Was it a racial thing? Levtov didn't think so. He had worked with a number of black students before—albeit on the minor tragedies—and this sort of tension had never surfaced. Maybe there was something about Jabari Frazier that was more elemental—or more threatening? In any case, the play was in big trouble, and Levtov knew it wasn't just a matter of accents and dialects.

He left for home feeling dispirited and defeated. The dismal fortunes of the play and the antagonism of its lead actor were weighing on him, of course. But Levtov sensed there was something else at stake, something else in play— just beyond his full awareness, like a lightening flash dimly glimpsed but barely heard. He sensed that there was something vital missing in him—and that whatever this was, it infused the very life-substance of Jabari Frazier.

Levtov tried to recall the last time he had felt deeply connected to his own governing spirit—what the ancient Stoics called *hegemonikon* and thought of as the seat of the soul. There were, of course, the formative years at Cornell, when life seemed sweet and fertile and infinite. There were the first few months of Joel's life, when Adam cradled the tiny bundle of possibilities in his arms, envisioning the great poet-scholar-scientist the Blessed Boy inevitably would become.

The answer came to Levtov in a flood of remembered joy and buried longing. He was ten years old, hunting for fossils in the still-vacant lots behind his house on Naramore Drive. Nearly 400 million years ago, during the mid-Devonian period, the area now called western New York was covered by a vast, inland sea. In prehistoric Batavia, a gigantic coral reef teemed with life, including the prolific trilobites—those small, three-lobed creatures prized by amateur rock-hounds like the young Adam Levtov. On a good day, armed only with patience, a keen eye, and the requisite tools of the fossil hunter—hammer, chisel, and brush—a boy might discover a treasure-trove of brachiopods, gastropods, crinoids and corals. Young Adam would rise on a jewel-bright, October morning; watch his breath condense in the chilled, morning air; and head out to unearth the ancient sea-trove—and especially, the mysterious trilobite. The rest of the world would fade to gray: the hectoring of his father; the burden of homework; the dull recitations and translations of Hebrew school. And a blue, cloudless horizon would open before him.

Now, that lucid sky seemed as remote from him as the mid-Devonian period. Whatever life-force had coursed through the fossil-hunting boy—whatever sweet link to earth and heaven he had felt—that ancient sea had evaporated long ago, leaving only the residue of a vanished world.

*   *   *

Chapter 10

No me dejen morir!

It was easy to say how the fight began, but harder to understand why it persisted well into the night. How do fights between husband and wife usually begin? A simple observation like, "You seem a little irritable tonight, honey" may be the tiny seed that causes all the salt in the supersaturated solution to precipitate, yielding copious heat—a reaction that old Mr. Burnham, Levtov's high school chemistry teacher, had called "exothermic crystallization." Thus, the seemingly simple question, "Any more thoughts about our family situation, Bec?"—in reality, not a simple question at all—had provoked a battle royal between Adam and Rebecca.

In the heat of such a conflict, it is easy to forget fundamental historical facts; for example, that Adam Levtov had fallen in love with Rebecca Kornbluth within an hour of encountering her in the stacks of Cornell's Uris Library, where the two of them had made out obliviously until well after midnight. (*Yes, yes*—the "love at first sight" trope is justly prosecuted as clichéd, but Adam Levtov was prepared to testify in its behalf). It was early October, 1989, and the first, red battalions of maple leaves had massed in Cascadilla Gorge—an emblem of the brightness and possibilities of their lives. In the salt-in-wound sting of argument, it was easy to forget that this same Rebecca Kornbluth had been the love of Adam Levtov's life; and that, to this day, he felt a pang of longing whenever her hazel eyes flickered from brown to green, in the day's changing light. Under such conditions, he could refuse Rebecca nothing. It is easy to forget such facts when the brain is sodden with loss and hurt and anger.

"Any more thoughts about our family situation, Bec?" Levtov thought the question innocuous, or at least non-inflammatory. But what had led him to ask it in the first place? He reflected on this while lying in bed, restless and ruminating, later that night. Earlier that day, Levtov had noticed that his dark, curly hair had been thinning—not only on the crown of his head, but also in front, where he had enjoyed an exuberance of curls since boyhood. To make matters worse: that same morning, after his shower, Levtov had noticed some enlargement in his pectoral region—a fatty sagging around his nipples that instantly called forth the jejune term, "man-boobs." This had alarmed him, and he had done a quick "Google" search on the nature and treatment of gynecomastia and pseudogynecomastia. The search had revealed a corrective surgical procedure called "mastopexy", which had struck Levtov as a kind of medieval mutilation. From his days reading Greek classics, he recalled the figure of Teiresias, the blind prophet of Thebes who had been transformed into a woman. In grad school, Levtov had chuckled over Apollinaire's surrealist play, *The Breasts of Tiresias*—a title that did not seem nearly as funny now.

"*Nu*, darling," he could hear his mother asking, eyebrows raised and hands extended, "what does all this breast *mishugas* have to do with you and Rebecca fighting? Or with having another child?"

Levtov could hardly offer a confident reply. But he suspected some connection between his denaturing body and a bizarre dream he had experienced, the night before the big fight. It involved, of all things, the last words of Hugo Chavez—the late President of Venezuela—who had died of cancer earlier in the year. Rumor had it that, in his last minutes of life, Chavez had mouthed the words, *"Yo no quiero morir, por favor no me dejen morir!"* "I don't want to die. Please don't let me die!" In Levtov's dream, it was he—Adam Levtov—who was lying on his death bed, as the thuggish face of Hugo Chavez stared down at him, grinning malevolently.

Levtov chuckled into his pillow, hoping he had not awakened Rebecca. Any good comp lit major could tease out the themes of flagging masculinity and encroaching mortality, in these recent events. And in strife's quiet aftermath, Levtov began to glimpse, though only dimly, how these ancient archetypes might have fueled his quarrel with Rebecca. But at the time of their row, he could do little more than whine and yawp in Neanderthal rage. As Levtov reconstructed their interchange, it had gone something like this:

> He: I'm just saying, Bec, it would be wonderful to have another kid. I know there are risks, but . . .
>
> She: Risks? Jesus, Adam, I'm forty-three! Who'd be taking the risks? And then, who'd be taking care of Sweet Baby Levtov? Somehow I can't see you stepping up to burping, bathing, and butt-wiping!"

"Come on, Bec, that's not fair! I helped out with Joel. You remember—you'd be working late at the office, and . . ."

"Yeah, you helped out when it was *convenient*, like in between grading papers! Adam, please listen! Instead of wishing for a new kid on the block, why, for God's sake, don't you start loving the son we have?"

"Whoa, wait just a goddamn minute, Rebecca! That's not fair! I love Joel and you know it. It's just that he—with all this Gothic bullshit . . . ."

"Have you ever asked Joel if he feels loved by you, Adam? Ever wondered about that?"

"Well, no—I mean, not in so many words, but . . . ."

"Jesus, why do think the kid wears my fucking eye liner to school? Why do you think he practically makes out with Seth Greenberg? Because he feels loved by *you*?"

"Oh, for Chrissake, Bec, now you're hitting below the belt! You're gonna blame me for . . . I mean, if Joel is really gay . . ." His voice had broken, much to his shame—broken just like Joel's voice.

In questioning her husband's love for Joel, Rebecca had administered what Esther Levtov, the rebbetzin, would have called a *klung*—a punch in the teeth so hard, you could hear bells ring! Adam could scarcely appreciate it at the time, but his wife was dealing with her own fears and losses—the dreaded double chin, for starters, as well as the slow mortification of her father's once magnificent mind. And then, the idea that, at forty-three—the notion of burping and bathing another child? Ridiculous!

But at this point in their altercation, Adam and Rebecca were startled by the sound of sneakered feet tromping up the stairs, followed shortly by a brutal, cracking noise. A strange chordal undertone accompanied the commotion, closely followed by a hair-raising yowl from Pupik, who came tearing down the stairs in panicked flight. For a moment, the quarreling couple froze. At first, they thought that Elie had tipped over his book shelf again, but quickly realized that the cacophony had come from Joel's end of the upstairs hallway. They exchanged stricken glances and bounded up the wide, mahogany staircase to the second floor. They found the door to Joel's room locked and heard the infernal rhythms of Bauhaus blasting from behind his bedroom door. In the foyer, they found the smashed remnants of their son's acoustic guitar, shattered to pieces against their hand-carved, Victorian armoire.

*   *   *

Chapter 11

Recalled to Life

The next day, Joel would not come out of his room, even for breakfast, and had taped a sign on his bedroom door, reading, "This Freak Won't Speak!" Adam and Rebecca had made several entreaties, all to no avail, and the boy's door remained locked. Fortunately, it was Saturday, so school was not an issue—but the couple's plans to attend a chamber music concert at the college were now ruined. Marisol had come in to care for Elie, but she couldn't be expected, in addition, to deal with "Joel's little Hamlet act," as Adam described the boy's behavior. Levtov recalled Act 2, Scene 2 of the play, when Claudius asks Rosencrantz and Guildenstern to cheer up the melancholy prince: *I entreat you both/ That, being of so young days brought up with him/ . . . To draw him on to pleasures and to gather/, So much as from occasion you may glean/, Whether aught, to us unknown, afflicts him thus/ That, opened, lies within our remedy.*

Where were R & G when you needed them? Levtov grumbled silently, fuming about the scrubbed concert plans. And what was the remedy for the boy's fit of pique? Of course, Levtov understood how, overhearing the quarrel between Rebecca and him, Joel had become upset. Whether he had actually overheard his sexual orientation being discussed was unclear—but it seemed plausible, given the timing of the guitar-smashing. Setting aside the issue of the pulverized, Victorian armoire—Adam and Rebecca had purchased it at an antique show, for $1900—Levtov could not abide the boy's jejune, passive-aggressive behavior.

"What did you expect, Adam?" Rebecca said to him as they strategized in the kitchen, sipping coffee. "You never got pissed off at your parents when you were fifteen, and hunkered down in your room?"

"Well, yeah, maybe I did for an hour or two, when my father was ragging on me. But we didn't say anything to Joel that would have . . ."

"It's what you said *about* him, honey, and the way he thinks you *feel* about him. You need to talk to him, Adam."

"Hey, wait a minute, Bec! You were the one who said Joel was practically making out with Seth, and that . . . ."

"*Shhh*!" Rebecca interjected adamantly, finger to mouth. "OK, OK, I admit it! Maybe Joel overheard what I said, too. I'm sorry! We can both sit down with him, honey. But I really think Joel needs to hear from you. I think he thinks you *hate* him. I know that's not true, but . . .

"OK, I get it, Bec! The kid's got a persecution complex! I'll have a talk with him."

But Joel refused to speak with Adam. Repeated knocks on the door produced only silence—or rather, the cacophony of Siouxsie and the Banshees, unmitigated by human speech. At one point, Levtov had a sudden pang of anxiety—what if Joel did something stupid, like hurt himself? Maybe they should force the door open? But then, mercifully, even through the din, Levtov could hear his son chatting on his iPhone, apparently to Seth. The boy's conversation was laced with derisive laughter and references to "dickheads,"

"Abercrombies," and "the same old shit." So it seemed there was no emergency.

Suddenly, Levtov had a flash of inspired desperation. He walked briskly down the hallway, past the shattered armoire—as yet, the shards of mahogony had not been cleared away—and knocked on the door to Elie's room.

Marisol opened the door and greeted Levtov with a nervous smile.

"*Buenas tardes*, Señor Adam! I am so sorry you and the Señora not hear the concert. But *Papi*—I mean, Señor Elie—he is doing OK today. I straighten the room for him, and give him little sponge bath. Oh—and I meant to tell you . . . . there was a man who came to see you . . . ."

But by this time, Elie Kornbluth had called out, "Adam, my dear, is that you? Please, please, enter my humble abode!"

"Marisol, let's talk later, OK?" Levtov said abruptly. "And thanks for taking such good care of Elie. I had better go in now and see him."

The old man seemed in good spirits. His illness was like that: one day, one hour, he could be calm and welcoming, with tinges of the Old Professor still evident in his emotional complexion. Another day, another hour, and he was ready to tear around the neighborhood, feeding their good steak to the dogs—or singing Yiddish folk songs at the top of his lungs. Some days, Elie would spend hours standing in front of the mirror with one of his old, silk ties wrapped loosely around his neck, trying repeatedly to tie a good, shapely Windsor knot—alas, a ceremony of futility.

Levtov recalled the paper he had found on the internet, describing fronto-temporal dementia—one of the diagnostic possibilities Elie's doctors had considered—with its plethora of symptoms: everything from apathy to euphoria to "childish excitement." But was any of this within the old man's control?

On a good day, did the august, Professorial Will rise up, Lazarus-like, from the old man's dead and dying neurons—or was it all a matter of random electrical impulses? Levtov could hear his father quoting Talmud, over the dinner table: "Man is always fully responsible—*mu'ad*—whether he causes damage intentionally or unintentionally, whether awake or asleep!" This proposition had always seemed implausible to young Adam, who understood it as his father's rationale for administering punishment—particularly since the Hebrew read, "*adam muad l'olam.*" Imagine, having your given name form part of a Talmudic tongue-lashing! In any case, this afternoon—*knock on wood!* as Levtov's mother would say—Elie Kornbluth seemed like his old, genially imperial self.

"Ah, and to what do I owe this honor, my dear—your kind visit to my study?" Elie crowed, extending his hand to his son-in-law. Though he stood there in his yellowed, terry-cloth robe, stained by God knows what bodily secretions, Elie Kornbluth still possessed the regal demeanor that had so unnerved Levtov, nearly a quarter century ago.

"Well, Pop, to be perfectly—I mean, this isn't easy for me to talk about, but . . ."

"Oh, come, my dear! "*Give sorrow words*; *the grief that does not speak* . . . ehm, that is . . . *the grief that does not speak* . . ."* For a moment, the Great Man faltered, struggling with a quote known as intimately to him in his teaching days as his own street address. Then finally, the words came: "*. . . the grief that does not speak knits up the o-er wrought heart and bids it break.*"

"Thanks, Pop. Fortunately, things aren't quite as bad for me as they were for Macduff! But, well—Bec and I have been having some, um, problems with Joel. I'm sort of hoping you might be able . . . . that you might consider talking to him. He seems to relate to you in a way . . ."

"Oh, yes, of course, my dear! He's a sweet boy, Joel. A bit perplexed, I think. Did something upset him? I hope it was nothing I said?"

"No, no, Pop! I think you're the one Joel feels most comfortable around. Your Shakespearean broadmindedness, I guess. Bec and I were, you know—arguing the other night. I think he might have overhead us and . . . or maybe I just haven't learned how to relate to him. Anyway, he won't come out of his room—won't even answer when we call to him. We're starting to get a little worried. If you could just talk to him—and maybe get him to come out . . . ."

Levtov watched as Elie Kornbluth drew himself up to his full height. For the first time in a long time, the former Sterling Professor of the Humanities and English was not being sponge-bathed or restrained or patronized. He was being called to duty. He spoke to his son-in-law in a voice he himself had nearly forgotten.

"Young Joel shall not all alone beweep his outcast state, my dear. You shall see!"

* * *

Chapter 12

The King of the Fairies

It was early Saturday evening, and the mid-October sun had set with a blazing flare of red and saffron. Marisol had left for the day, and Adam had been tasked with bringing home a pizza for dinner. Rebecca thought her husband had been perturbed by something Marisol had said, just as Adam was leaving—something about "a man who came to the house the other day." Meanwhile, whatever Elie had said to Joel, his words clearly had their intended effect. With no explanation, the boy had padded downstairs, still in his pajamas, and now sat at the kitchen table, sipping a glass of orange juice.

"So, I'm sorry about the—you know, the antique, Mom," he said without looking at Rebecca. "I'll find a way to pay you guys back."

"We can talk about that later, honey, after your dad gets home," Rebecca said, putting her arms around Joel from behind. "I'm more concerned right now about what—I mean, why you smashed your guitar, and . . ."

"Mom, can we just not talk about that now? I had a good talk with Zayde, and I'm, like, all talked out!"

"OK, Joel, that's fine. Um—do you mind, though, if I ask you what Zayde talked to *you* about? You know, honey, even though he's sick, he's still my Dad, and I love . . ."

At this point, Rebecca had to bite her lip in order to keep back the tears.

"It's OK, Mom," Joel said, putting his hand on his mother's wrist, "I know it's hard, watching your own father so sick and stuff . . . but, Zayde was really cool with me. I mean, he sounded almost like the old Zayde, like, before he got sick."

"That's really great to hear, honey. I'd love to hear what he said to you, if that's, you know, comfortable."

To Rebecca's surprise, Joel's face lit up, as he flipped a stray curl off his face. "Yeah, Mom, that's cool. Zayde was like, "Let's talk about Shakespeare, my dear!" You know how he gets when he's excited. So he starts telling me about this play, "A Midsummer Night's Dream." I guess Dad knows it really well, but I've never seen it or read it. In English class, we did *Macbeth* this year, but that was it. Anyway, Zayde starts telling me about this dream play, you know? And it's about—I had to laugh my butt off, Mom!—this dude, Oberon, and his wife, um . . . Titania. And Oberon is King of the Fairies, and Titania is Queen of the Fairies!" At this point, the boy let loose a high-pitched cackle. "I mean, how gay is *that*? I know the fairies weren't, like, drag queens or anything. They were magical and stuff. But Zayde said—I'm trying to remember his words—he said that Shakespeare had "very fluid gender boundaries." And he said that, in Shakespeare's day, all the girls' parts were played by guys, you know, in drag. And one of the fairies, Puck, he's kind of—whaddya call it?—andro . . . androg . . . ."

"Androgynous?" Rebecca chimed in, smiling nervously. "Yeah, that's right, honey. Your dad and I once saw a production in New York, and the part of Puck was played by a woman. But other times, it's played by a man."

"Yeah, and Zayde said that Shakespeare was kind of, you know, maybe gay or bi, or something."

"Well, Zayde knows Shakespeare better than anybody alive, even though his memory isn't what it used to be. Hey, but—can I ask you something, honey? In school—I mean, I know you and your friends like the goth stuff, dressing up in special clothes, and all that. That's all fine, Joel—I mean, as long as you don't get into trouble with the principal again! But—are you OK with the other kids? I mean, do they tease you or bully you, or . . ."

Joel looked down at the table and scowled, his hands balled up in tight fists. "Well, some of the kids at school are definitely dickheads! They get right into your face sometimes and call you, you know—messed-up names. Or do gross stuff to your locker. I'm OK, though, Mom. You don't need to worry. I'm not gonna, like, shoot up the school or anything!"

Rebecca's face went white. "Oh, honey, no, God no! That's—I wasn't even imagining . . . I just want to know if you are happy with—well, with *who you are*. Or would it help to talk with somebody . . . ?"

"Like a shrink? Mom, no effing way, please! I'm OK. I mean, I'm still trying to figure out what I want, or what I am, exactly. The other night with the guitar—I was just pissed because I heard you guys say something about Seth and me, and then I heard Dad say that I'm gay and . . ."

"Oh, Joel, no—I mean, Dad didn't actually say that. He's just not sure . . ."

"Well, I don't like being talked about, that's all! And maybe Dad should mind his own fucking business and figure out why he's always so pissy around me! I mean, for as long as I can remember . . ."

Rebecca interrupted. "Oh, I know, honey—I think it's other things that are bothering your dad. Things that don't have anything to do with you. He and I—you know, we've been talking about whether we should have another kid, and . . ."

"Mom, are you shittin' me? I mean, no offense but— you're gorgeous and all, but aren't you a little . . . um . . . ?"

"It's alright, honey, you can say it! Yeah, I *am* a little old, though I could do it, I mean biologically, I could have another baby. But I'm not at all sure I want to, what with Zayde and my work and all. But your dad, he . . ."

Suddenly the front door opened with a clatter, and a rush of cool, October air pushed into the kitchen. "Pizza's here!" Adam Levtov called out cheerily. For Levtov, pizza had always been the great family mediator—the centerpiece in their ceremony of feeding and healing. He could still recall Joel, at age five or six, bounding down the stairs in his pajamas, eager to participate in the adult ritual of gobbling down the hot, cheesy, crusty mess. For Joel's eighth birthday, Adam and Rebecca had hired the chief pizza maker from Hope Falls Pizzeria, who had delighted Joel and his friends by spinning the raw dough and tossing it into the air, in fine, theatrical fashion. It hardly seemed possible that seven years had gone by—and it pained Levtov to acknowledge how far apart he and his son had grown.

But now, as Adam set the large box down on the kitchen table, only Rebecca was there to greet him. She gave her husband a stricken look and squeezed his hand in commiseration. "You just missed him, hon," she said softly, blinking back a tear. "You just missed him!"

*   *   *

Chapter 13

Strike While the Irony is Hot

Levtov pulled into the college parking lot with five minutes to spare before rehearsal, but his mind was 4,600 miles away—roughly the distance from Hope Falls to Moscow. He had finally found time to speak with Marisol regarding the man who had come to the house, while he and Rebecca were out.

"He was a *beeg* man with a funny accent, Señor Adam!" Marisol had said, her brown eyes widening with concern. Levtov had smiled and raised his eyebrows with gentle irony. "I know, I know, Señor Adam," Marisol said with a good-natured laugh, "I speak like I just step off the boat from San Juan! But this man—he sound like, you know, the Russian spies in the James Bond movies!"

At first, Levtov had been slightly amused by Marisol's description. But as she filled in a few details, his mood darkened. The man, it turned out, had come to the house in the late afternoon, looking for "Professor Levtov." He had been polite, but insistent, wanting to know when the professor would be home. Marisol, to her credit, had kept the chain lock fastened on the front door as she spoke with the man, and had given him no information. She described him as tall, in his late thirties or forties, with a Van Dyke beard, and "built like the bull." He had refused to leave a calling card or any information, but indicated that he would "be in touch."

"You know, Señor Adam," Marisol had added in a kind of stage whisper, ". . . . this man, he was like—we say in Puerto Rico, *como perro que huele carne*—he was like a dog that smells meat!"

At that, Levtov had felt a familiar prickly feeling on the back of his neck, which he had come to associate with the scrawled letters from Ignatieff. But Grigory Ignatieff, by now, would be a man in his late seventies or early eighties—not the robust, middle-aged man who had showed up at the house. Naturally, Levtov's mind turned to the cinematic and sinister: was the man a KGB agent? Russian mob? A goon sent by Ignatieff to intimidate him—or worse? His mind quickly ran through a series of protective scenarios: he could call the police, buy a gun, hire a bodyguard—or maybe move the entire family out of town. But that would be nearly impossible, given Elie's needs. Even calling the police seemed a gesture of futility, given that there was no clear threat to report. "Officer, a big Russian man came to my door and asked to see me!" did not seem likely to spur the local police into action—particularly in light of Elie's unbridled forays into the neighborhood, which had not endeared the Levtovs to Hope Falls's Finest. There was really nothing to do except caution Marisol, Rebecca, and Joel to remain vigilant, and to call the police if the man came round again.

As he headed down the corridor to his office, Levtov noticed Ivor Somerset waving from the other end of the hallway. It was not a conventional, "How are you doing?" wave; but rather, a kind of mocking, finger-wiggling wave. Levtov associated the gesture with the subway scene in "The French Connection," when the drug smuggler, Charnier, waves goodbye to "Popeye" Doyle, whom the villain has just eluded. But before Levtov could investigate, Somerset had slipped hurriedly into his own office and closed the door.

When Levtov entered the performance chamber, he expected to find the usual gaggle of student actors milling about, chatting on their cell phones or flirting with one another. Instead, the lead actors sat sullenly on the stage, looking as if someone had just cancelled spring break.

"OK, you guys, what's up?" Levtov called out breezily. "Somebody's dog die, or what?"

Jabari Frazier—all 6 foot, 2 inches of him—stood up on the stage, and folded his arms. At first, he looked down at his feet, as if he were saddened or ashamed at what he had to say. But then he lifted his head, and met Levtov's gaze straight-on.

"Professa Liftoff," he said in that deeply resonant voice, "with all due respeck, we are hereby officially on strike." Nods and mumbles of "That's right!" issued from the mouths of Brittany Kendrick, Josh Altshuler, and Heather Schultz. Levtov thought he heard, "*Fahkin-A!*" from Shaun Brannah.

Levtov laughed. "OK, I get it. It's a strike. Great joke, guys! Now can we get to work on . . ."

"It's no joke, Professa," Jabari Frazier said calmly. "We been talkin', all of us—and then we got some advice from Professa Sum'set."

At this, Levtov suddenly felt his stomach turn. His voice quavered despite his best efforts. "You . . . you were talking with Ivor Somerset? About *our* play? What the hell—I mean, why . . . why didn't you guys speak with *me*, if you had a problem?"

"Professa Liftoff," Frazier said almost plaintively, "We *did* speak witchoo, man! We kept sayin' how we had to do this *our* way, speak our parts the way we used to speakin.' But each time we came to you . . ."

But Levtov, by this point, was barely able to contain his rage. It was not directed at the hapless student actors so much as at Ivor Somerset—who, evidently, had put the students up to this and had given Levtov the "French connection" wave as a way of rubbing his face in the imbroglio.

"OK, OK, excuse me, guys!" Levtov broke in, carefully modulating his voice. "I need to leave for a little while. I'll be back soon, and then we'll discuss the situation."

Levtov left the performance chamber and stormed down the hall to Ivor Somerset's office. Struggling to contain his anger, he knocked on Somerset's door, then—before any response could be given—burst into the small office. To Levtov's surprise and considerable embarrassment, Somerset was sitting calmly at his desk, sipping a cup of tea, while Creighton Fitchly sat in one of the two plush, leather chairs, kitty-corner to Somerset.

Levtov was at a loss. "Oh, I . . . . I'm sorry," he stammered. "I didn't realize . . . good to see you, Creighton! I had meant to speak with Ivor, and . . ."

"Please have a seat, Adam," the Chairman said with a decided edge in his voice. "I've been speaking with Ivor, and I think perhaps we should all have a chat. You see, I'm really very distressed by this Othello debacle."

At this point, Somerset spoke up. "Yes, I'm quite distressed, too, Adam. Naturally, I didn't intend to spring anything on you, old chap! But just before you arrived, four of your little urchins button-holed me in the hall and begged for my sage advice. It seems your band of brothers and sisters are not at all happy with how you've been running things."

"That's really not your business, Ivor!" Levtov said with more force than he had intended, feeling the blood pounding in his temples. "If there's a problem with my actors . . ."

"Adam," Fitchly interrupted, raising his hand to Levtov, "Please excuse me. But this . . . this "strike" by your students—it is really unprecedented in all the years I've been at Hope Falls. You know very well that *Othello* is the department's biggest production this year. I have already invited the Dean and several visiting department heads to the premiere, not to mention Mrs. Fitchley, who is a huge fan of the play. And with the date only a few weeks off, well—I'm afraid that this may indeed have to become Ivor's business."

"Sir?" Levtov said, his voice cracking. "I'm not sure what you are saying. Do you mean that Somerset . . ."

"I mean, Adam, that if you can't get your little brood back under your wing and ready to rehearse within the next few days, I'll have no choice but to turn the production over to Ivor."

Somerset shifted in his chair and cleared his throat, struggling to suppress what Elie Kornbluth would have termed a *risus faecivorus*—in the parlance of Levtov's college days, "a shit-eating grin."

*   *   *

Chapter 14

I am not what I am

Levtov did not think much about God—at least, not in the way his father the rabbi would have wished. On a good day—an autumnal, blue-sky, fossil-hunting day—Levtov was prepared to believe in some beneficent, all-knowing and all-powerful Deity. On a bad day—when Elie was howling and Joel was barricaded in his room and Adam and Rebecca were fighting over the future of Rebecca's uterus—Levtov could scarcely credit the existence of such a being. Never mind, the Holocaust and 9/11: *prima facie* refutations of anything in the cosmos remotely resembling a just and loving deity.

But Levtov did think a good deal about mortality—about the preposterous evanescence and microscopic insignificance of his own life. Lately, he had also pondered the legacy he might bequeath those who came after his interment. What would he leave that would do mankind, or even a solitary, searching individual, any possible good?

Once, Levtov had high hopes of becoming a playwright. No, he did not expect to be carved into the Mount Rushmore of Playwrights, along with Beckett, Albee and O'Neill. But he did imagine that his work would survive a few decades, before being effaced from what Faulkner called "the wall of oblivion." Now, even this did not seem a likely prospect.

After all, his smash-hit play, "Lustig the Tummler," was partly fraudulent. It was clearly just a matter of time before the theft would be discovered—particularly since the victim of the crime, or one of his goons, was already hot on Levtov's trail.

So, for many years, Levtov had taken up a fall-back position on the mount of mortality, hoping that, as a professor and drama teacher, he might make a mark—maybe even shift the course of some young lives a few degrees. But—shift them to *what*, exactly? Levtov once had imagined that exposure to the great works of drama—Shakespeare, Chekhov, the pantheon of American playwrights—might favorably alter the course of his students' journey through life. Now, this seemed risible and foolish. To be sure, a handful of students were filled with passion and longing, but their brains were addled by the numbing effects of American pop culture, high-potency pot (much more so than in the days of the Howie Herskowitz hash brownies), and the self-indulgent narcissism that pervades American society.

And there was a rootlessness in today's students that seemed more pronounced than when Levtov was in college—a disconnection between their own lives and the rich soil of myth and meaning, cultivated in other eras. When you asked today's deracinated college students to reflect on Jungian archetypes or Platonic forms or Elizabethan literature, you were met with a look of bovine perplexity—like the expression Levtov had encountered once, when a huge, spotted cow blocked his way on a hiking-path in the Swiss alps.

Then there were the endless faculty meetings, grant applications, lesson plans, and committee obligations—and of course, the primal struggle for tenure. The drudgery of academe had tugged Levtov's aspirations downward, much as the gravity of a black hole bends nearby light rays. Yet in his bones, he knew—though he kept such dark knowledge at a safe distance—that these complaints were mostly a self-comforting salve. It was not the drudgery of academe, or the failings of his students, that explained why he hadn't written a single new play in the fifteen years since *Lustig the Tummler*. Nor was it anyone's fault but his own that his production of *Othello* was now on the cusp of catastrophe.

And as for marriage and family—what did he have to show for it all, after twenty years of courtship, commitment, and conception? A wife—a kind, beautiful and intelligent wife, to be sure—at odds with him over the life, or non-life, of the child who might or might not be; a son whose every breath seemed to inhale sorrow and exhale pain; and a demented father-in-law who howled Yiddish songs while pissing into the sink. As his mother would say, rolling her eyes, "Other than that, Mrs. Lincoln, how did you like the play?"

Thus, Levtov's rank ruminations, sitting at his computer at 7:56 p.m., waiting for Rebecca to return after a late night at the office. He had just eaten a dried-out chunk of leftover lasagna and was preparing to do some writing, when an idea occurred to him: he would ask the Dean of Shakespearean scholarship for a bit of advice. True, the Dean's mind was not what it once was, what with a thousand amyloid plaques choking off those brilliant brain cells. Still, Levtov reckoned, the old man probably had more working neurons than the average corporate CEO or university department chair.

Levtov knocked on Elie's door, which the Great Man always kept closed—a boundary he had insisted on for as long as Elie had known him, and which had resisted even the onslaught of dementia.

"Enter!" came the booming baritone, sounding its usual theatrical note.

Elie was sitting on his bed with Pupik, gently stroking the cat's head. A contented *purrrr* issued from the petite, gray creature, whose eyes seemed glazed over with a kind of intoxicated pleasure. Over the years, the old man had developed a peculiar affinity with the capricious cat, whom he often called, "My dear Graymalkin" or "my familiar." In Elie's company, Pupik's aggressive behaviors seemed to melt away. Oddly enough, Levtov had observed that Elie's periods of "disinhibition" abated when Pupik was by his side.

"Ah, Adam! To what do I owe the honor of your visit?" Elie said, rising suddenly to his feet, as the startled Pupik scurried under the bed.

"Well, Pop, to be honest—I could use a little of your professional advice."

"Well, then, of course! Please, my dear, have a seat and I will do my best!" For the moment, at least, the old man's face—relaxed and radiant—seemed almost that of the man Levtov had revered more than twenty years ago.

"Well, for starters, I'm having a problem with my *Othello.*"

Levtov explained the debacle that had developed with his student actors: the problems with their diction; the confrontation with Jabari Frazier; and finally, the ignominious strike, engineered by that ophidian fop, Ivor Somerset. With only two weeks to go until the dress rehearsal, Levtov needed some kind of miracle, lest Creighton Fitchley turn the whole thing over to Somerset.

To Levtov's surprise, Elie Kornbluth listened for nearly ten minutes without saying a word. He seemed, at times, to be in a kind of trance or meditative state, with a vague smile on his lips. Then, suddenly, a look of sadness crossed his features, and the old scholar sighed deeply.

"Ah, my dear, I'm sorry to hear of your woes! When I was a young assistant professor, in my early 30s, I made the same mistake you are making. I was directing a production of *Macbeth* at Yale, and I kept pushing the actors to sound like Elizabethans! Of course, back then, there was a more traditional view of Shakespeare, and many American actors thought they needed to sound like Larry Olivier. Oh, dear old Larry! Did you know, my dear, that Olivier loved kippers? Yes, yes that's right—smoked herring! I, of course, prefer smoked whitefish, as you and Rebecca well know. Oh, Olivier once made a terrible scene over his beloved kippers! How do I know? Why, it was in—let me see, 1964, aboard the *Brighton Belle*, bound for London. Yes, you see, I was in my mid-twenties, and studying theater with the wonderful Peter Hall, at the Royal Shakespeare. It happened I was on the same train to London as the great Olivier—and actually wound up sitting near him in the dining car. Oh, yes—I'm quite serious, my dear! The great man nearly went apoplectic when the steward told him they had run out of kippers! And, oh, the sultry looks that man gave me! No, no, not the steward, my dear—Larry Olivier! Ah, but I digress. My battered brain cells winking out! But to continue, Adam: it is a great mistake to fight with your students over their diction. They will simply come to detest you, even if they wind up sounding like Sir Philip Sidney. What's that you say? The young black man playing Othello? Ah, let him be, my dear, let him be! You know, some scholars believe that the American southern accent is fairly close to that of the Elizabethans, though the claim is hotly disputed. But, believe me, you will do much better with your actors if you leave their native accents unvarnished and unpolished."

Levtov rose from his chair, beaming, feeling as if a tight iron band around his chest had been cut free. He was about to thank his father-in-law for his sage advice, when Elie suddenly raised his hand, as if to stop Levtov from speaking.

"Adam, my dear, please," he said softly. "Please sit down. I hope you don't take offense, but—I feel obliged to ask you something, for your soul's sake—and maybe for the sake of your safety. Please forgive an old man's meddling, but—what do you intend to do about your *Tummler* play?"

Levtov felt the blood drain from his face and fought off a feeling of nausea. "Pop, I don't even know . . . what do you mean, "do about" the play?"

"Oh, my dear, please don't make this more painful than it already is, for a beef-witted old man! You know, that time you and Rebecca visited me—in the mid-90s, I think—after you left the house, I found the copy of Ignatieff's play, still open to Act 3, lying on the reading table in my library. No, my dear, I'm afraid you are not a very clever thief! And, of course, I was a great admirer of Ignatieff—I still am!—so that when your "Tummler" play came out, I was stunned. There I was in the audience, in New York—and I was mortified! And all these years—you have kept this from everyone, poor fellow, except your conscience."

Levtov struggled to keep his voice from cracking. The blanching of his face had now been replaced by the deep flush of shame. "Pop—I don't know what to say. And, I don't understand—if you knew all this on the day of the premiere, why didn't you say something to me then? And why have you waited all these years to . . . ?"

"Oh, my dear!" Elie broke in. "Surely you don't imagine that I would have ruined your great off-Broadway triumph on the very first night! Besides, I wasn't entirely certain—I *was* something of a scholar, you know—so I had to go back home and compare your third act to the text of Ignatieff's play, including the original Russian version. And then—well, for many years, I hoped against hope that you might come forward yourself and perhaps explain how you could have . . . well, you understand the delicacy of exposing one's own *son-in-law*, surely, Adam! And, of course, after you and Rebecca generously took me in, I was hardly in a position—well, as it were, one feels beholden . . ."

"Yeah, I understand that, Pop. I can't even begin to tell you how ashamed I am to—I mean, you know how I idolized you, and built my whole career on your scholarship. And now, to have you think I'm just a big, fucking fraud who . . ."

"Oh, no my dear, don't do that to yourself! The play—your "Tummler"—was really brilliant! You never needed Ignatieff's work at all! You could easily have pulled it off yourself. No, dear Adam—my aim in bringing this up now is not to shame you. I raise it now—well, before I lose the entirety of my cerebral endowment, I wanted you to know that I have been worried about you these past few years. And I am especially worried about Joel. He is such a dear, sweet boy, you know—with so much promise. And I see him drifting farther and farther away from you, Adam. That episode—when was it? Last month?—when the poor boy locked himself away! Somehow, I think it all stems from what you have put yourself through, in all the years since your play. I can't quite explain how, but I think it all has to do with your problems with poor Joel."

Levtov had grown very quiet, sitting with his head between his hands. He ran his fingers through his hair, and spoke in a voice barely above a whisper.

"I don't know, Pop. I honest-to-God don't know. Maybe you're right—I don't know why Joel and I don't connect. I mean, partly, it's all that Goth nonsense, the bleached hair, that God-awful music—but I know it goes deeper than that."

Elie Kornbluth rose and walked over to his son-in-law, placing his hand on Adam's shoulder. "Yes, I'm sure it does. Well, my dear, remember: 'Many things have fallen, only to rise to more exalted heights.'"

"Hmmm . . . Shakespeare? I don't know that one, Pop."

"Oh, no—that's Seneca, my friend across the centuries. Even now his stoicism is a consolation to me—balm for a hurt mind, if I may mangle *Macbeth*. But, Adam, listen—I *know* this Ignatieff! I met him once at a conference in St. Petersburg. He is as tough as old Russian army boots! He will eventually discover your theft, if he hasn't already. Yes, he's quite old, like me—but he will not rest until he has put things right. So I ask you again, my dear—*what do you intend to do?*

*   *   *

Chapter 15

O true apothecary, thy drugs are quick

The call came from the school nurse, and was first picked up by Marisol. Marisol—barely able to contain her panic, and reverting to a mixture of English and Spanish—relayed the message to Rebecca, who was in Syracuse, tied up in a meeting with the partners. Levtov's cell phone rang just as he was to meet with Creighton Fitchley, regarding the *Othello* debacle. Rebecca had tried her best to sound composed, but her voice had quavered with fear, and finally broke, with the words, "Oh, honey, he took some kind of overdose!" After profuse apologies to his department chair, Levtov drove twenty miles to the Onondaga General ER, in under eighteen minutes, speeding through Manlius and thanking God that a local police cruiser had turned off the road, just ahead of him.

According to the school nurse, Joel had been acting peculiarly in English class. He had seemed a bit giddy; his speech was somewhat slurred; and he appeared to be dozing off, despite a sharp, "Levtov! Straighten up and pay attention!" from Mr. Bruckner. After Joel slid from his seat onto the classroom floor, Mr. Bruckner carried the boy over his shoulder to the school nurse's office. Old Jane Cosgrove— with thirty years at Hope Falls High under her belt—took one look at the boy, checked his blood pressure and pupils, and immediately called 911.

When Levtov arrived at the ER—which was packed with wheezing asthmatics, caterwauling infants, and sniffling druggies coming down off their heroin highs—Rebecca was already standing in the hallway, speaking with the doctor. She caught sight of Adam and waved him over to her, grabbing his hand and squeezing it tightly.

"He's OK, honey," she said, smiling through her tears, "the doctor says he'll be OK."

The doctor looked no older than some of Levtov's students, except for a deep, M-shaped furrow between his eyebrows. "Uh, it looks like your son swallowed five or six antihistamine tabs, judging from what we got back after we lavaged him," he said in an affectless monotone. "That's consistent with stupor, slurred speech and the like. Do you guys have, like, some Benedryl at home, in the medicine cabinet?"

Adam and Rebecca exchanged anxious glances, fearing they were about to be scolded. *And what is it*, Levtov wondered, *with the use of "guys" as a universal, unisexual form of address? Whatever happened to "Mr. and Mrs. X", or maybe the more congenial, "you folks"?*

"Uh, yeah, I think we do—for allergies," Levtov offered meekly.

"It's OK," the doctor continued. "I'm not pointing fingers or anything. I just want to see if there was anything Joel might have taken at home. Also, we're gonna need a psych consult before he can leave. Anyway, his vitals are stable now, so if you want to see him, he's in bed number 7."

Joel was drowsy, but smiled when he saw his parents pull back the curtains. The head of his bed was cranked up, and an IV line dripped slowly into his arm. A cardiac monitor beeped out the boy's heart rate, and displayed his blood pressure as "100/70". In the next bed, an elderly Hispanic man was muttering, over and over, *"Por favor, m'ija,* just let me go!"

"Hey," Joel said weakly, "I'm really sorry. I don't know . . . I mean—I'm sorry to put you guys through . . ."

"Shhh, honey!" Rebecca interrupted, "It's OK! You don't need to say anything right now." She ran her fingers through the boy's dark, curly hair, musing that his blond streak seemed oddly faded.

But Joel seemed eager to speak, as if to relieve some inner sense of pressure.

"It wasn't a big deal, really. I mean, I took a few of those pink allergy tablets from the medicine cabinet, you know. It's all because—there were a couple of jerks in school who posted—they put up a video on YouTube . . . of me! And I kinda over-reacted, that's all. I'm OK now, really. When can I go home?"

Levtov leaned in closer to his son. "Joel, what sort of video? What do you mean? On YouTube?"

"Dad, it's no big deal—just some stupid video of me walking down the hall in school. They doctored it to make me look, you know, like I was wearing a dress and stuff. I got pissed off, and . . . ."

Rebecca interrupted angrily, "Honey, who are these little shits? Do you know who did this? This is sexual harassment—it's cyber-bullying, for god's sake! And that almost certainly violates the terms of service established by YouTube or . . . ."

"Mom, please, don't make a federal case! I don't wanna lawyer up! I just want to forget this and go home."

"Joel," Adam said gently, "they're gonna have another doctor talk to you first. You know, just to make sure . . ."

"Oh, Jesus, a fucking *shrink*? Mom, Dad—please, I'm OK! I wasn't trying to—I just got fed up with it all!"

"You know, Joel," Adam said a bit plaintively, "you could have come to talk with one of us. I know you and I haven't been on the best of terms, but still . . ."

But the boy would have none of this. "Oh, yeah, *right!*" he said, his voice cracking. "Like I'm gonna consult *you guys*, after what you said about me, that night!"

"What night?" Adam asked heatedly. "The night you smashed our $2000 armoire to pieces? Jesus, Joel, you can't just try to kill yourself and then shrug it off with . . . ."

"I wasn't trying to kill myself, Dad! Can't you hear anything I say? Jesus!" Joel was now in tears.

By this time, a nurse had come back to check on the loud commotion, and gently chided Adam and Rebecca. "OK, folks, I'm gonna need you to quiet things down back here, OK? We don't want to upset people resting back here, do we? Can I get you some juice out in the reception area? I think it might be better if you let our young man here rest up and not upset him, OK? And in a little while, Dr. Feinman will stop by and speak with your son."

"I'm not talking with a fucking shrink!" Joel said, tossing a plastic cup from his bedside table.

But before this matter could be settled, another nurse appeared by the bedside, and announced, "Excuse me, there's a young man out in the waiting area who is asking to speak with Joel Levtov. He says it's important, and I'm wondering if . . ."

"It's *Seth*!" Joel said excitedly. "Tell him, well . . . Oh, tell him I'd like to speak with him. Mom, Dad—would you please give us a little time alone?"

Adam and Rebecca exchanged puzzled glances, and Rebecca looked slightly hurt.

"Honey, we know Seth. Why do you need us . . . I mean, you really want us to *leave*?"

"Yeah, please, Mom. It's nothing against you guys—I just . . . I need to talk with Seth alone is all."

Rebecca and Adam sullenly withdrew to the hospital cafeteria, where they gorged themselves on overcooked cheeseburgers and soggy fries, and talked about their son's brush with death—though later that night, after an internet search, Adam learned that five or six 25-mg tablets of diphenhydramine did not constitute a lethal dose. So perhaps Joel had made what some people call a "suicide gesture", without an actual wish to die? An hour later, this is essentially what they would hear from the consultant psychiatrist, Dr. Feinman, who authorized Joel's discharge late that afternoon.

"So, your son is a pretty angry kid, and he has some serious identity issues to work out," Feinman had informed them, "but he doesn't want to die. The overdose was a message to you, and maybe others, that Joel wants help. I think this video thing is just the tip of the iceberg, but Joel wasn't ready to get into the deeper stuff. In the short term, I don't think he is at a high risk of repeating this, and I think it's safe for him to go home. But someone should keep an eye on him for at least the next 48 hours. And I would strongly recommend psychotherapy for Joel—maybe some family counseling, too. This sort of thing isn't easy on parents, and you might both benefit from some therapy. And, feel free to call me if you have any concerns about Joel's safety."

What Feinman had not discovered—because Joel had taken great care to conceal it—was that the offending YouTube video had appeared more than two weeks ago; and, although very upsetting, was not the immediate precipitant of

Joel's overdose. What neither Dr. Feinman nor Joel's parents had discovered was that, one day prior to his overdose, Joel had seen Seth Greenberg flirting with Jess Henry, just outside the gym at Hope Falls High.

*   *   *

Chapter 16

A Rainy Night in Georgia

It seemed the strike was over. Levtov, taking Elie Kornbluth's advice to heart, had made a fine speech before the "Gang of Five"—Kendrick, Altshuler, Schultz, Brannah, and Frazier. He apologized for what he called his "imperial attitude" and promised to allow the actors full discretion in the matter of their accents. This prompted another "*Fahkin A!*" from Brannah, and loud whoops from Kendrick, Altshuler and Schultz. But from Jabari Frazier, there was only statuesque silence.

"Yo, Professa Liftoff," Frazier said, stepping down from the stage. "You got a couple minutes?"

"Uh, yeah, of course, Jabari. Let's go to my office." Levtov was perplexed by Frazier's sullen demeanor. He felt queasy as he escorted the young man into the cramped space that passed for an office.

"Please, sit down, Jabari. Cuppa coffee?"

"No thank you, Professa." The young man shifted uneasily in his seat and clenched his jaw. "Uh—with all due respect, I need to tell you something, man. I can't—I can't do the play. I will not play Othello."

Levtov's face went ashen, and his guts lamented with their usual mourning dove *coo*.

"What . . . Jabari, I . . . what the hell? What do you mean 'you won't'? We have two weeks before opening night! I thought the strike was over. I told you guys, you don't have to worry about your accents. So what's going on?"

Frazier attempted a smile, but produced something more like a smirk.

"Man, I heard your little Henry Five jive speech. *Oooh*, we all jus'a happy band of brothers, right? But see, I know your game, Professa. You don't have to be no Einstein! I've seen it my whole life. It all comes down to *respect*."

At this point, Jabari Frazier stood up and began pacing around the small office, seeming to fill the entire, eight-by-eight space. Levtov felt the hairs on his neck stiffen.

"You think the way I talk is nothin' but mistakes with the King's English, right, Professa? But it's not like that with you and *Brannah*, is it?" Frazier said, his voice tight with anger. "You hear Brannah and you think, OK, here's a kid from South Boston with a Southie accent. *Fahkin-A*! That's cool, you know—like, Matt Damon in "Good Will Hunting!" But you hear me, and you think, here's some dumbass kid from Georgia who doesn't *know* any better. And, man, that is *wack*, you know what I'm sayin'?"

Levtov felt his face flush with shame. "No, Jabari, that's not how I feel! I understand that AAVE—you know, African American Vernacular English—it's not "wrong" in any linguistic sense. It's a perfectly legitimate variant of standard . . ."

But Frazier interrupted with a sardonic laugh. "Yo, Professa Liftoff, it's OK, man! I know you not a racist! You don't have to sell me the liberal line. But, it's like, you think I can't speak any other way . . . or maybe, that I can't *think* any other way."

Levtov sat in sullen silence. But at that point, Frazer stopped pacing, and his face seemed to relax slightly. Slowly, a smile emerged. "Hey, Professa, tell me something—you ever hear of Queen Latifa?"

Levtov was flummoxed. He had some recollection of a movie star or singer—a black singer, he thought—but he was not at all sure about this particular "queen."

"Uh, you'll have to refresh my memory, Jabari."

Frazier laughed. "Yeah, I figured! OK, see, Queen Latifa, she's a sista who can do a *perfect* British accent—I mean, like Masterpiece Theater English! When I was a kid, I used to love hearin' her do this real hoity-toity accent—and I could do it right along with her! Don't look so surprised, man! We had TV sets down in Georgia! And I used to listen to James Earl Jones, too. You know what? James Earl Jones was born in Mississippi, and he was a stutterer. But he overcame it. And the man winds up doing Othello in that deep-down-in-the-well voice of his. That's how I first got interested in theater! So—you want to hear me do Othello in the King's English, Professa? OK, then—listen up, man. Act 3, Scene 3."

Jabari Frazier suddenly seemed to rise a few inches above his already towering height. His facial expression, roiled earlier by hurt, anger and sarcasm, now reflected the bitterness of a broken general and the shame of a cuckold. Frazier spoke thus:

> *"O, now, for ever*
> *Farewell the tranquil mind! farewell content!*
> *Farewell the plumed troop, and the big wars,*
> *That make ambition virtue! O, farewell!*
> *Farewell the neighing steed, and the shrill trump,*
> *The spirit-stirring drum, the ear-piercing fife,*
> *The royal banner, and all quality,*

> *Pride, pomp and circumstance of glorious war!*
> *And, O you mortal engines, whose rude throats*
> *The immortal Jove's dead clamours counterfeit,*
> *Farewell! Othello's occupation's gone!*

Levtov listened as if to the revelation at Sinai, his mouth gradually forming an astonished "O." The voice was recognizably that of Jabari Frazier, but one easily might have imagined a young Olivier, or perhaps a Lawrence Fishburne, reciting the lines from Othello.

"Holy shit!" was Levtov's awed and ineloquent response.

Jabari Fazier smiled. It was not an arrogant smile, but one that might have appeared on the face of a well-satisfied district attorney, making his closing argument. "So, Professa, you see what I'm sayin'? If I wanna sound like James Earl Jones, I can do that. If I want to sound like Lawrence Fishburne, I can do that. But that's not what I'm about, man. What I do as Othello—that comes from in here!" Frazier thumped his breastbone with his closed fist. "And if you don't trust what I have on the *inside*—man, I'm not gettin' up on that stage!"

Levtov struggled to find his footing. He felt like a man clinging to a slick rock face, suspended a mile above a deep canyon.

"Jabari," he began. "That was—that was a magnificent recitation. I'm sorry for giving you the idea—for focusing so much on accent and diction. You're right—a performance comes from the inside out, and I know you have what it takes, deep inside. Otherwise, I would never have picked you for Othello. We may not be a happy band of brothers, and, God knows, I'm no Henry V! But we *need* you, Jabari—the players need you, and so do I. Will you please stay with us?"

Frazier seemed to ponder the question for a minute. He walked to the office door, turned toward Levtov, and smiled broadly. "I'll take you up on that coffee some time, Professa Liftoff."

*   *   *

Chapter 17

On With the Show, This Is It!

Levtov wiped the sweat off his forehead and cursed softly, pacing like a caged lion. Backstage, the ventilation was so poor, most of the actors had to wipe their brows with cold washcloths, in between entrances. Remarkably, Josh Althsuler—a.ka.a. Brabantio—was on his cell phone, apparently closing some sort of deal. Heather Schultz was adjusting her push-up bra, creating the impression of a "Lady in Waiting" waiting to make the beast with two backs. Only Jabari Frazier seemed in possession of both himself and his role as the Great General, standing with his arms folded and his brow knitted in fierce concentration.

Levtov had seen the audience file in, and knew that the front row of the tiny performance center—demarcated by "RESERVED" signs—was occupied by the Brahmins of Hope Falls College, such as they were: Creighton and Agatha Fitchley, looking like stuffed, matrimonial owls; Marcus Aurelius Davenport (D. Litt. Oxon), Dean of Arts; Mary Catherine Krawczyk, Dean of Students and Brian Tierney Professor of Medieval Studies; and, of course, Prof. Ivor Somerset and his wife, Olivia, whose throat-clearing habit seemed exacerbated by sitting in the crowded theater. Somerset himself sat quietly, wearing the sort of salivary expression one might expect from a fox anticipating a fine old night in the hen house. To Levtov's immense irritation, Rebecca somehow had been seated next to Somerset, despite having been instructed by her husband to sit next to Agatha Fitchley. Was it Levtov's overwrought imagination, or did Ivor Somerset already have his hand on Rebecca's knee? With the stage lights glaring, it was impossible to be sure.

The play unfolded before the extremely taciturn audience. Given the myriad uncertainties of the past few months, Levtov was prepared for the worst—but his actors did not let him down. Brittany Kendrick—she of the "Entry In Rear" tattoo—managed to convey Desdemona's wounded innocence, even unto death. Shaun Brannah—having mastered the bard's iambic pentameter and dulled the sharp edges of his Southie accent—was deliciously serpentine, as Iago. As for Jabari Frazier, the audience could not have been more in thrall, as he spoke his lines in a rolling cadence that somehow melded rural Georgia with Elizabethan England. As Creighton Fitchley was to comment, after the performance, "That young man must have been channeling Paul Robeson—a giant of the woods in the great hurricane of tragedy!" The transported audience gave Jabari Frazier three curtain calls. Even Ivor Somerset, looking vaguely disappointed, came backstage to congratulate Levtov.

"Well, dear boy," he said, leaning in so close that Levtov could smell the liquor on his breath, "you didn't make a bollocks of it, after all! No, no—in truth, it was bloody marvelous!" And at that point, to Levtov's astonishment, Somerset planted a wet kiss on his cheek. Then, as Somerset pulled away from the flummoxed director, his expression suddenly became grave. "By the way, Adam," he said in a conspiratorial stage whisper, "Our Rebecca looks *remarkably* fit these days!" When Levtov looked puzzled, Somerset roared with laughter, slapped Levtov on the back, and pranced off with a slightly ataxic gait. Only after a few minutes of reflection did Levtov recall that "fit", in British slang, conveys something along the lines of "fetching" or "sexy". And Somerset's insolent "*Our* Rebecca" brought blood to Levtov's face.

The faculty and cast were to meet at a nearby pub for celebratory drinks, and there was a good deal of congratulatory laughter and backslapping, backstage. Levtov had expected to see Rebecca in the wings, but he looked around for her in vain. Suddenly, he found himself gently but unmistakably backed into a corner by a man who must have been at least Jabari Frazier's height, but with twice his bulk. Formally attired in a black dinner jacket, and sporting a neatly-trimmed Van Dyke beard, the interloper gave the impression of a Mafia hit-man masquerading as a diplomat. When the man began to speak with a heavily-inflected Russian accent, Levtov realized with a shudder that this was the "*beeg* man with a funny accent" Marisol had encountered—the man who had come looking for Levtov at the house.

"Good evening, Professor Levtov," the man said, showing a set of unnaturally white teeth. "May I congratulate you on excellent performance! I almost wish my father had been here to enjoy it."

"Um, uh, sorry," Levtov stammered, "you are *who*, exactly?"

The man chuckled and bared his radiant teeth. "Oh, come now, Professor! I am sure you can guess who I am, given my father's many letters to you, which of course have gone unanswered. Ah, but I have been ill-mannered—*nyet kulturny*, as my dear father would say!"

The man extended an impeccably manicured hand, the size of a catcher's mitt. "I am Alexei Ignatieff, and I am here as the legal representative of my father, Grigory Ignatieff. My father has requested a meeting with you at your earliest convenience, Professor, which really means . . . . well, tomorrow afternoon. My father is staying with me in Syracuse, but I will be happy to bring him to your office. Would 2 p.m. work for you, Professor? No? Not so well? Ah, a pity! May I then respectfully suggest you *make* it work, Professor!"

This suggestion was said with teeth bared, in what otherwise could have been a smile. And with that, Alexei Ignatieff withdrew his hulking presence so quickly, and with such leonine grace, Levtov could scarcely believe his eyes. Suddenly, Rebecca was standing next to him, smiling broadly.

"Mazel tov and kudos, Mr. Director!" she said, beaming, quickly planting a kiss on Adam's cheek. But Rebecca's expression suddenly changed. "Hey . . . what's the deal, hon? You look like you just saw Banquo's ghost!

"Worse, Bec," Levtov replied in a quavering voice, his lips trembling. "Much worse! But can we talk about it after the party?"

*　　*　　*

Chapter 18

Riddling Confession

Adam and Rebecca made a brief appearance at Del Vecchio's Pub, just off campus, but Adam was hardly in a partying mood. After a round of drinks, a brief schmooze with Creighton Fitchley, and a pat on the back for each of his actors, Levtov pleaded "post-dramatic stress disorder", grabbed Rebecca's arm and hustled out to the car. Thankfully, they had managed to avoid the seriously inebriated Ivor Somerset, or there might well have been a row.

Levtov had never revealed his act of plagiarism to his wife, or indeed, to anyone, notwithstanding Elie Kornbluth's astute uncovering of the crime. But now, as they drove home, Rebecca was peppering Adam with questions: "Who was that bear of a man buttonholing you, backstage? What did he want? And why did you look like a blanched raisin, after he finished talking to you? What the hell is going on, Adam?"

"Oh, god, Bec," Adam sighed, "it's a long, sad story. And not one I'm proud to tell."

"Listen, hon," she replied, placing her hand on his shoulder, "whatever it is, we'll deal with it. And—I mean, if there's some kind of legal issue involved, you know I'm happy to help with that."

Levtov smiled and, unexpectedly, felt his eyes welling up. This was the same Rebecca Kornbluth who had seen the family through so many troubles, these last few years: coping with her father's breakdown; getting Elie settled in to their home and seeing to his medical needs; and, of course, dealing with Joel's *meshuganeh* Goth rebellion. This was the ever-so-careful lawyer, who always reinforced her "sticky notes" with a piece of cellophane tape, lest the adhesive fail. Levtov felt a sudden twinge of guilt—how could he suspect this good, true and steadfast woman of a dalliance with that serpent, Ivor Somerset? At the very least, she had better taste than that. Now, after fifteen years of concealment, it was time to confide in his wife. Levtov had just opened his mouth to speak, when his cell phone went off. It was Marisol, and she sounded upset.

"Señor Adam, I am so sorry to bother you on the big night! No, no, everything is OK with Señor Elie—but I am worried about Joel. He stay in his room all night and is very quiet. When I knock, he say, "Marisol, leave me alone!" Señor Adam, I know this boy since he was ten, and I have the bad feelings he needs to tell you something."

Instinctively, Levtov stepped on the gas. "Jesus, Bec, Marisol thinks something is up with Joel. That's all we need, right? Let's hope he's not thinking about doing something stupid again, for Chrissake."

"Well, hon," Rebecca said gently, "I think there's more going on with Joel and Seth Greenberg than he's saying. And I have a feeling we had better hear him out on this."

"You think . . . . ? I mean, that Joel and Seth are . . . ?"

"I don't know, but I know that something is bubbling up in our son that needs to be heard, and that we need to listen without, you know . . ."

"Yeah, I get it. Sensitive, caring. The whole fucking deal!"

"Jesus, Adam, I don't know why you always sound angry whenever we talk about Joel! It's like—there's some part of you that just has to smack him down, and I . . ."

"Look, Bec, I haven't smacked him down! I've tried to live with his goddamn Goth music and his pansy Goth fucking clothes, and . . ."

"Adam! Listen to yourself! Who or what are you dealing with? Joel or—maybe something's going on with you that you need to . . . ?"

"Well, OK, alright! Yeah, I'm basically screwed, Bec! That gorilla in the dinner jacket who came backstage—he's the son of a Russian playwright. A man named Ignatieff. And, well, it's a long story, but . . ."

Rebecca was silent for the next five minutes, fiercely working her jaw muscles as Adam spoke. She listened to her husband describe how his big, off-Broadway success, "Lustig the Tummler", was actually a gigantic fraud—how nearly the entire third act was lifted from Grigory Ignatieff's comic masterpiece; and how, after fifteen years, Ignatieff had tracked him down, sent him dozens of letters—including one to Levtov's mother!—and how, with his son as his proxy, Grigory Ignatieff was insisting on a meeting tomorrow.

At length, Rebecca spoke. "Holy shit, honey. I mean, *holy shit*! How on earth could you have kept this . . . ?" She paused to collect herself and suppressed her feelings of outrage and betrayal. She resumed in an even, lawyerly voice. "OK, Adam, look—does anybody else know about all this?"

"Yeah, Bec—your dear, demented father, who still has more working neurons than most of my colleagues. He figured the whole thing out long ago. But he never said anything to anybody."

Her husband *and* her father had kept this a secret from her? For—what?—fifteen years? Rebecca compressed her lips and fought off the urge to cry. She responded, instead, in a manner befitting a senior partner at the law firm of Malamud, O'Brien, Freund and Levtov.

"OK, honey, let's think this through. Has the guy's son said anything about any legal action? Has he or his father threatened you in any way? Who is supposed to be at this meeting tomorrow? I could come as your legal representative, and . . ."

"Bec, please! I've caused enough trouble already, and I don't want to drag you into this shit! Nobody has threatened me, at least not, you know, explicitly. I think I need to meet with this guy—with Grigory Ignatieff—and see what he wants. I'll be in my office and there will be plenty of people around. Please, Bec—just let me handle this. I'm gonna need your help a hell of a lot more in dealing with Joel."

*   *   *

Chapter 19

The Master-Mistress of My Passion

When they got home, Marisol was already in the front foyer, her brow deeply furrowed. Pupik padded up to Adam and Rebecca, produced an alarmingly loud *meeoww* and rubbed her head briskly against Rebecca's ankle.

"*Ay, dios mio!*" Marisol said, putting a hand to her forehead, "I am so glad to see you both! Señor Elie, he is fine, I just give him sponge bath and now he goes to sleep. But Joel, he won't even answer me now, from behind his door. I hope he is OK, but after what happened, you know—with the pills . . ."

Levtov sighed and took off his coat. "I'll go up to check on him. Thank you, Marisol, for keeping an eye on everybody."

"Um, hon, I'll go with you," Rebecca said immediately, trying to conceal her worry that Adam's seeing Joel alone might make things worse.

Rebecca determined that she should be the one to knock on Joel's door—"I think he'll find it a little less threatening," she said to Adam—and he concurred without protest.

"Leave me alone!" was the surly and predictable response from behind the door. Oddly, this had a reassuring effect on both parents—surly being infinitely better than comatose, or worse, and well within the realm of their usual, familial *sturm und drang.*

"Honey, please," Rebecca pleaded, "We're not here to scold or criticize—just to talk. *Cross my heart and hope to dine!*" This little family joke sent a pang of sorrow knifing through Rebecca and Adam. When Joel was in first grade, he had heard the expression, *"Cross my heart and hope to die!"* from one of his school friends, Manny Ziskin. The reference to death had frightened the boy, and he had asked his parents, "Does this mean Manny is going to die?" Rebecca had reassured her son that, no, Manny wouldn't die—and that Joel's friend had been trying to say, "Cross my heart and hope to *dine.*" This benignly misleading security patch had worked well at the time; and, as Joel came of age, the "dine-line" evolved into a running gag for the Levtovs. Whenever Adam or Rebecca wanted to assure Joel of their good faith—like the time they promised a skeptical, ten-year-old Joel a trip to Disney World—the bastardized expression would be trotted out, accompanied by a parental hand placed solemnly over the heart. (The family did indeed do Disney World, notwithstanding a two-hour line for "Pirates of the Caribbean").

There was a minute of anxious waiting, outside Joel's room—then the door opened.

"Honey," Rebecca said, wrapping her arms around her son and fighting back tears, "I'm so glad . . . I'm so glad . . ."

Levtov gave his son a quick pat on the shoulder, and mussed the boy's blond-streaked hair. "Good to see you, kiddo!" he said, averting Joel's eyes. He fought off that familiar but terrifying feeling he had experienced intermittently for the past fifteen years—the sensation of transparency that left him wondering, at times, if he was truly a creature of flesh and blood.

"So, Joel," Rebecca said, regaining her composure, "Marisol called us and sounded a little worried about you. She said you weren't coming out and . . ."

"Mom, Dad," Joel interjected with an urgency in his voice, "it wasn't the video! It wasn't the goddamn video!" At this, the young man flung himself onto his bed, causing the bed frame to groan ominously. He buried his head in his hands and began to sob softly.

"It's OK, Joel," Adam said in a frail and quavering voice, provoking a look of concern from Rebecca. "Let's talk about it, OK? What do you mean, it wasn't the video? *What* wasn't?"

"The pills, the fucking pills!" Joel mumbled miserably, struggling to sit up in bed. "The video they made about me—that was weeks before I took the . . . the video was just bullshit. Stuff I'm used to, like dealing with the Abercrombies."

"So, honey," Rebecca said, settling herself on the bed, and placing her hand on Joel's shoulder, "what was going on for you before you, you know . . . took the pills?"

Joel shook his head, as if trying to dislodge some water from his ears. "I don't know if I can tell you. I don't know what you'll think or say if . . ."

"It's OK, Joel," Adam interjected, "we love you, kiddo. And you can tell us anything." But in his heart, Adam felt an ice pick of dread. Was Joel about to blame *him* for what had happened—for ruining his young life and nearly driving him to suicide? Adam suddenly had the impulse to run out of the room and grab Elie, who had some kind of strange, bewitching rapport with the boy. Elie, with his oceanic heart and Shakespearean soul—so much better equipped to play this scene than was the pitiful director of minor tragedies!

Rebecca decided to go with her intuition. "Joel, honey—did what happened with the pills—did it have anything to do with your friend Seth? I know he came to the emergency room to see you, and . . ."

At this, Joel lifted his head and gazed into his mother's eyes. His breathing became rapid and shallow, and his lip trembled.

"Mom, Dad—Oh, god, how do I say it? I . . . I think I love Seth! And—the day before I took the pills, I saw him, like—you know, coming on to this other kid. This total *asshole*, Jess Henry! And it all just scares—it all scares the shit out of me!" At this, the young man put his head on his mother's shoulder and began to sob.

"Shh . . . shhh . . . it's OK, honey. Everything is going to be OK," Rebecca said, rocking her son slowly in her arms. Levtov walked over to the two of them, placed his arms around them and melded into their rhythmic swaying. He said nothing, but for a few moments, he felt solid again: a creature of flesh, a creature of this world. He was, once again, the boy who hunted fossils on a sunny day, in the remnants of a Devonian sea.

*　　*　　*

Chapter 20

Let everything happen to you

Levtov sat at his desk, drumming his pencil, waiting for the call from Gwen Wallace, the department secretary. Gwen also handled Creighton Fitchley's secretarial tasks, and had been with the department for twenty-five years. At five-feet four, in her early sixties, with a build like that of the smiling Buddha, it was easy to underestimate Gwen Wallace—at one's peril! She claimed descent from the great Scottish hero, William Wallace, who defeated an English army at the Battle of Stirling Bridge—and nobody in the department dared challenge this genealogy. Most of the faculty credited Gwen with "running the place", in as much as Creighton Fitchley—a superb scholar—had the administrative skills God gave crab apples. Junior faculty who got on Gwen Wallace's bad side soon discovered just how miserable life in the department could be—including but not limited to hours searching for those mysteriously misplaced salary checks. Levtov could usually tell from Gwen's voice whether a matter was routine, urgent, or—as was usually the case—transcendently forgettable. And so, at precisely 2 pm, when Gwen's voice sounded slightly breathless over the phone, Levtov knew there was cause for concern.

"Adam, um, there are two men here to see you. They, well, they say they have an appointment. One of them is an old guy, the other is, uh, sort of a big, friggin grizzly bear. And they have funny accents. Do you want me to take them down to your office?"

"Uh, yeah, thanks, Gwen. It's OK—I'm sort of expecting them. You can walk them down. But just to let you know, there may be reason to alert security, if you hear any, well, loud noises."

"Well, OK, Adam, but—security today would be Henry Halloway, and you know Henry. He's going to Upstate next week for a total hip replacement. I'd allow about fifteen minutes' response time to any screams or shrieks."

The knock at the door came a minute later, and, standing outside his office, Levtov found himself confronting the old man and the grizzly bear. Or perhaps "Mishka"—Russia's huge yet agile brown bear—might have been a more appropriate moniker for the hulking Alexei Ignatieff, who seemed ready to burst the seams of his double-breasted suit. The old man said nothing to Levtov, but made a quick, dismissive gesture toward his son. "Alexei," he said firmly, "*pozhaluysta, ostav'te nas v pokoye!*"

Alexei frowned. "Alone? But, father," the bear growled, "I am your official legal representative! I should be present for any . . ."

"Please, Alexei!" the old man interrupted, raising his hand to close off discussion, "I wish to have civilized talk with Professor. Legal we do later. And now, Professor Letov, please permit me to introduce." Grigory Ignatieff extended his hand and bowed slightly. "I am Grigory Ignatieff, author of play, "The Comic." I believe this work is to you quite familiar, *da?*"

"Yes, sir," Levtov replied, grasping the old man's gnarled hand, "quite familiar. Please, please, come into my office." Levtov's stomach did a double-flip and produced its characteristic mourning dove *coo*.

The old man gently lowered himself into the chair catty-corner to Levtov's desk and scanned the tiny office as if searching for hidden cameras. Grigory Ignatieff was not a bear of a man, like his son, but nonetheless had a massive presence that instantly commanded attention. Dressed neatly but casually, in dark blue trousers, an open shirt, and a brown, corduroy jacket, Ignatieff gave the impression of a Chekhovian satyr. He stood nearly six feet tall—a good three inches above Levtov—and had the bulk of a man once powerfully built, but now given over to a comfortably well-fed rotundity. His silver-grey hair glistened with what Levtov took to be some sort of pomade. His ruddy face was ornamented by a bushy, gray goatee in the European style, and one could almost imagine Anton Chekhov's *pince-nez* clipped to the old man's nose. Instead, he wore a pair of round, wire-rim glasses, through which he peered with dancing, mischievous eyes.

Levtov offered Ignatieff a cup of coffee, but the playwright politely declined. "At my age, heart is not so happy with coffee," he said, patting his sternum. "Balls are going, too!" he said with a low, insinuating growl, pointing toward his crotch. At this, Ignatieff let loose a loud guffaw. "Used to be, when I was your age, I have wife and mistress. Three nights of week, sex with wife; two nights, fucking mistress! Always walking around with *stolbniak*, you know? *Erektsiya*. What is English for this—"hard on"?"

"Um, uh, yes, that's erect," Levtov said, blushing. "I mean, *correct*, if I understand you, sir." Levtov was flummoxed. He had been preparing himself for a dressing down, a donnybrook, or at least an unpleasant shouting match. Yet the man before him seemed effervescently friendly, if not a bit hypomanic (a term Levtov had learned from Elie's neurologist).

Suddenly, Ignatieff's expression darkened and the bubbly demeanor of just a few moments ago went flat. "So, my dear professor, you know why I am here, no?"

"Well, I think I have a pretty good idea, sir."

"Please, not to use "sir." Call me Grigory! I know in my letters I sound wery angry. I try on purpose to put some fear in you, so that you *listen* to me, so that you meet with me, Professor . . . ."

"Please, call me Adam."

Ignatieff smiled, showing a full mouth of yellowed teeth. "*Ochen' khoroshiy!* Wery good! We speak playwright to playwright. May I ask, please, Adam, you are how old?"

"I'm about to turn forty-six."

Ignatieff sighed. "Ah, I am old enough to be your father! I am now seventy-six."

At this, Levtov was slightly taken aback. In fact, his own father would have been seventy-five, had he not been dragged off in his fifties by bone cancer.

"I ask age because—well, because you have whole life ahead of you. But how will you use this life, Adam? That is question to ponder, no? Poets, artists, playwrights—we lay claim to *authenticity*, do we not? We are—how do you say?— *conduits* for some higher good. We speak for man's better angels. We claim inspiration from the Muse! But do we live authentic life for ourselves? I see now you look down at floor. I mean no offense, Adam. I don't wish to put you in shame. But, if I may ask—you have children?"

"Just one. A teen-age boy."

"Ah, like me—one boy! Plenty to keep us busy! My wife, she always wanted more children, but I tell her, my plays are my children. Alexei, he is good boy, a little younger than you.

He comes to America all on his own, twenty years ago, works his way through Cornell Law School—now he is—what you call?—"hot-shot" lawyer in Brighton Beach. But one child was enough! An artist must produce children that will outlast time, no? What did your Mr. Faulkner say? We want to leave scratch on "wall of oblivion," for someone a thousand years from now to see. And those spiritual children we produce— our writing, our plays, our works of art—they must be authentic, no? Maybe not immaculate—spotless is for the gods!—but still, *authentic*."

Levtov had been sitting nearly motionless, his arms folded over his protesting stomach, his head bowed. Now he felt obliged to speak.

"Grigory, I don't know what to say. I have no excuse for what I did, and I—I want to ask your forgiveness. I don't know why I did what I did, except that—maybe I didn't feel up to the job. I mean, up to writing "Lustig." And when I read your play, I thought the third act was just brilliant! Of course, I would be happy to compensate you for the money—I mean, any lost royalty income . . . and I apologize sincerely for the distress . . ."

Ignatieff made a dismissive swatting movement with his hand. "Enough! Your apology is accepted, Adam! And I know I made much worry for you in my letters. That gun business—just little joke! You see, real issue is not money, even though you stole from me third act of my play. I am not here to pick your pockets! It is matter of honor—and of *love*."

"I'm not sure I understand, Grigory. Honor, I get. But . . . love?"

Ignatieff smiled and seemed to blink back tears. "You see, Adam, I write my play, "The Comic," for my wife, Irena. She died one month after play is performed in Moscow, dedicated to her. Terrible death—from "melanoma." Same Greek word in Russian and English. Inside her eye, you know—the doctors could do nothing. But, my play, "Comic," was dedicated to her—to her laugh, her smile. She was beautiful, my Irena, and wery much loved life! Yes, yes, I know—you wonder how I can love wife and still have *lyubovnitsa*—a mistress!" Ignatieff shrugged and puffed out his cheeks, exhaling loudly. "In America, maybe this is strange—in Russia, mistress is wery common. For successful man, mistress is like trophy!"

Ignatieff clapped his hands together. "Well, to continue. So, in 2012, I come to New York and happen to see your play, "Lustig," at Second Stage Theater. Acts 1 and 2—for certain, Adam, *ya rassmeyalsya moyey zadnitsy!* I laugh my ass off! Then, I see act 3, and suddenly my heart feels like iron band is put around it. I sweat. My pulse races! I start having chest pain, because I see what you have done—steal from play I write for Irena, who is love of my life! I was in *yarost*—you say "fury", yes?—even though, I admit, I was also little bit flattered! But, my dear Adam—what I could never understand—did you not think your theft would be found out some day?"

Levtov slumped in his chair. "Grigory, I suppose, on some level, I knew I'd be exposed, eventually. In fact, my father-in-law figured it out right away. He is a big fan of yours, by the way. Do you know him—Elie Kornbluth?"

Ignatieff smiled and nodded vigorously. "*Da*, yes, of course! The great Kornbluth is father-in-law? I meet the Professor many years ago, at conference in St. Petersburg. He gave wonderful lecture on *Macbeth*, then we talk about Russian playwrights, over two bottles vodka! Your father-in-law, he knew my work—and also work of Andreyev and Denisov—very impressive man, very *kultúrny*! How is he, Prof. Kornbluth, these days?"

"Not good, I'm afraid. He has a very serious brain disease—a form of dementia . . ."

Ignatieff seemed stricken. "*Vey zmeer*! There is nothing to be done? I am so sorry, Adam—such a magnificent mind, Prof. Kornbluth! What? Ah, you are surprised I speak a little Yiddish. Well, I am mongrel, you see. On my father's side, I am descended from Count Nicholas Ignatieff. You would not know, but he was minister in the Czar's cabinet—a real *mudak*—an asshole! Persecuted the Jews, you see. But my mother, she was Jewess from Ukraine—a marvelous woman, and a fine poet, but never published. From her, I find my muse and pick up my Yiddish. And, of course, a Jewish mother means I am *Yid*, does it not?"

"Yes, yes it does, Grigory!" Levtov said with a laugh. "And somehow, that makes what I did to you, well—all the more painful."

Ignatieff smiled. "Well, after all, we playwrights—we do what we must, no? Shakespeare steals plot of *Romeo and Juliet* from poem by Arthur Brooke, who stole it from Italian poem! And, *po pravde govorya*—to tell the truth!—I might have stolen a scene or two from Ostrovsky's *Talanty y poklonniki,* for my "Comic". You do not know this work, by Ostrovsky? I am surprised—I bet your father-in-law knows! In English I think it is called, "Talents and Admirers." Anyway, stealing is part of our craft, no? But in the case of my play, you see—it was more than just the words. My "Comic" was written to cheer up Irena—to give her a little of the life we both knew she would never see. And so, Adam—I must ask you for more than apology . . ."

"I don't understand," Levtov said, shaking his head. "You said it wasn't a matter of money, and . . . ."

"*Nyet*, is not the money! What I want, Adam—I want you should give *credit*. Acknowledge Grigory Ignatieff and the love of his life—my Irena! Tell colleagues who it was really wrote third act of "Lustig!" Do this in public—so all the people know—and that will put matter to rest for me. Please, Adam, I am not young man. Please do this before I die!"

*　　*　　*

Chapter 21

The Winter of Our Discontent

Two months had passed since Levtov's meeting with Grigory Ignatieff. The gold and russet of October's foliage had long since disappeared. Now, in mid-December, an unexpected blizzard had dumped nearly three feet of snow on Hope Falls. Syracuse had been hit just as hard, with fierce winds sweeping across the warm waters of Lake Ontario and generating band after band of light, feathery snow. Giant plows with ten-foot blades prowled the roads, trying to keep up with the blinding squalls. The power had been out for two days in most of Hope Falls, and the emergency shelter at the college had taken in over fifty families. Adam's classes, of course, had been cancelled, and Rebecca's law firm had told its employees to stay home until the streets could be cleared. So the Levtovs remained hunkered down, their house swathed in white, sculpted drifts the size of sand dunes.

Unlike many of their neighbors, the Levtovs had power—and so, the house was abuzz with the blast of Joel's Goth music, the television's incessant weather updates, and the clicking of laptop keyboards. Yet for all the commotion, the gravity of winter seemed to tug the family's spirits into its immense, white field. Rebecca continued to work on pending cases and received the occasional, red-flagged "PRIORITY" email from the other senior partners. But she seemed distant and preoccupied, sometimes ignoring Adam's questions, or replying with a managerial, "Let's discuss that later, OK, hon?"

Joel had spent most of the past two days in his room. The boy had felt enormous relief in "coming out" to his parents, but was still reeling from Seth's betrayal. Oddly enough, the two boys had continued texting and had exchanged bitter profanities during one loud altercation over the phone.

Elie had become sullen and quiet, and seemed reluctant to get out of bed. He was having more trouble swallowing, and sometimes seemed to choke on his own secretions. Levtov had phoned his old friend, Gianni Chalakian, for a little medical advice, but the usually ebullient neurologist sounded subdued. "Well, Adam, if he has FTD—fronto-temporal dementia—you may be seeing the final stages of it," Chalakian had said. Rebecca had spoken with Dr. Stolberg, who warned her—unhelpfully—that, with prolonged time in bed, Elie could develop a blood clot or bed sores. The question of "home hospice" care had been discussed but quickly set aside by Adam and Rebecca, who seemed too enervated to deal with the issue. Meanwhile, strong, stalwart Marisol—who had trudged through hip-deep snow to reach the house—labored mightily to prod the old professor into action (*"Señor Elie, por favor, usted debe caminar!* You must get up and walk!"), but with little success.

Even Pupik seemed unusually languid, spending most of the day curled up on the couch and pawing listlessly at her food. Occasionally, she would scratch at the door of Elie's room, meowing miserably, until Marisol let her in. Then, the cat Elie referred to as, "My dear Graymalkin" would jump on to the professor's bed and curl up next to his chin, as he lay snoring with his mouth agape. Pupik would peer into the old man's mouth as if expecting a mouse to pop out of it.

Levtov wondered if something in the storm itself had depressed the family's mood. *Was it negative ions in the atmosphere that led to positive mood, or positive ions that led to negative mood?* He couldn't recall, and decided that a more parsimonious explanation lay in that old standby, "cabin fever." *Maybe we need such anodyne terms in order to avoid dealing with the real causes of our wintery discontent?* But cabin fever could not explain the return of Levtov's eerie feeling of translucency, which again seemed to inhabit him like some ghostly visitant. He had no insight into the genesis of this sensation, or why it had abated the night he and Joel and Rebecca had clung together in swaying communion.

Levtov had been ruminating over Ignatieff's plea—or was it really a kind of ultimatum? The old man had implored Levtov to come clean about the theft, but—technically— had not threatened any legal action if Levtov failed to do so. And yet, who knew what the playwright's son, Mishka the Bear, would do? No doubt, if Alexei felt it was in his father's interest to take legal action against Levtov, he would do so with little hesitation. Or maybe he'd rough Levtov up a bit—if not by himself, then through some Russian mob connections.

Adam had discussed the legal issues with Rebecca, shortly after his meeting with Grigory Ignatieff. Unfortunately, her considered opinion was that the Russian playwright would have a pretty good case against Levtov, if he wanted to press it.

"It falls under the rubric of copyright infringement, hon," she had explained to her husband, nervously tapping a pencil on the table. "The original author would be within his rights to sue, especially if the plagiarism resulted in a loss of profit for him."

"I think he just wants me to fess up, publicly, Bec. But what the hell does that mean? Get up on a soapbox and say, "I stole the third act of my play, "Lustig the Tummler" from Grigory Ignatieff, who had dedicated his own play, "Comic," to his loving wife, Irena?" Where and how would I confess such a thing?"

Rebecca wasn't entirely sure, and promised to consult with one of the "copyright guys" at her law firm. But so far, she hadn't done so, and Adam could only guess at her reasons for procrastinating. He had put off confronting Rebecca on this matter, suspecting that doing so might only exacerbate the tensions between them. After all, what kind of a sleazy schmuck of a husband plagiarizes from another writer and hides the whole business from his own wife, for fifteen years? *What in God's name was he thinking?*

What? indeed, Levtov thought, shaking his head. Rebecca had every right to be furious. It was not in her nature, though, to express her anger in fits of pique or pot-throwing. After all, this was the woman who, in open court, had stood up to the most obnoxious attorneys in Syracuse—most of them amply fueled by high-grade testosterone—and had never flinched. Over the course of her years at Malamud, O'Brien, and Freund—before her own name had been added to the firm—Rebecca Levtov had learned the fine, forensic art of turning anger into advantage. Once, when Old Man Malamud made a disparaging comment about Rebecca's work ethic—she had been five minutes late to a meeting because then three-year old Joel had spiked a fever—Rebecca had insisted on meeting with the firm's regal and intimidating founder. There, in his walnut-paneled office, which always reeked of stale cigar smoke, Rebecca not only confronted

Malamud about his unkind remark—eliciting a sheepish apology from the old man—but also took the opportunity to ask for a raise. Within a week, she got it.

So, no: there would be no throwing of pots and pans, over Adam's disreputable behavior, painful though it was to his wife. But in the past two months, Rebecca's anger and sense of betrayal had seeped out in more subtle ways. The radiant smile that usually greeted her husband was ever so slightly askew, as if Rebecca had just undergone painful dental work. The sparkle in her deep, hazel eyes seemed dulled by some imperceptible film. And in their lovemaking, Rebecca had seemed slightly distracted, as if pondering some leftover conundrum from the office.

There was yet another object of Levtov's wintery brooding. Ignatieff's disclosure that he was seventy-six— "old enough to be your father", was how he had put it—had opened a floodgate of memories for Levtov. His father, Rabbi Levtov, had died in mid-December, nearly a quarter-century ago. He had departed this world before he and his son could reconcile over the various animosities that had divided them, ever since Adam's teenage years. But the Rabbi had left his son a letter—the one that had been in the possession of Esther Levtov for more than twenty years. In the months since his visit to Florida, Levtov had avoided even close proximity to the letter, fearful of the sentiments it might reveal. It had remained sealed and tucked away in his home office desk drawer, under a pile of unread articles from the *American Journal of Theater Arts*. Now, finally, Levtov resolved to read it.

Chapter 22

Fathers and Sons

December 6, 1989
Dear Adam,

You are undoubtedly reading this some days or weeks after my death, unless, of course, something or someone has delayed your perusal of this letter. I hope that whatever stage of life you are in, you are healthy and happy. I am writing this to you, because, in my current weakened state, it would be too hard to speak these words—and because, truth be told, I am also a coward. You may find this an odd admission, and perhaps you have always thought of me as something of a bully or a pedant—an impression not without some factual basis. But for most of my adult life, I have been—first and foremost—a liar and a coward. A liar most of all to myself, but also to you and your dear mother, who put up with so much from me! She, who could have been a rabbi herself, in a just and righteous world!

I mean lying in the spiritual, not the factual, sense. You remember, Adam, the Talmudic teaching I used to pound into your poor head, over the years: "The Holy One hates him who says one thing in his mouth, and another in his heart." (Bavli, Pesachim 113b). Well, as I go to my grave, I can only hope and pray that *Hashem* will be merciful in His judgment of me, for I said many things in my mouth that were not in my heart. For twenty-five years, there I was, parading around as a rabbi, putting on holier-than-thou airs, when I never wanted to be a rabbi in the first place! You see, Adam, my father—whom you never knew—Rabbi Abraham Isadore Levtov (*z"l)*, wanted nothing in life so much as for his son to follow in his footsteps—and so I did, swallowing my duty like a bitter pill! In my mouth, I would chew and spit out words of high-minded holiness. But in my heart, I knew I was a fraud—and barely even a plausible fraud!

You know, Adam, what I really wanted to be was concert violinist. My idol, growing up, was not some great Jewish sage (though, of course, I admired Rambam), but Jascha Heifetz! Like our ancestors, Heifetz's family was Lithuanian, from Vilnius. (You may not know this, but our family name was originally Levertov. When my grandfather emigrated to the U.S., a customs official mistakenly recorded his surname as "Levtov"—instantly converting us, in Hebrew, to the "Good Heart" family!). Anyway, I am rambling—I suspect that the pain medication they have me on is affecting my thinking at this point. And even with the medication, the pain is very great.

I was starting to write that, all my life, I wanted to follow in the footsteps of Heifetz—but my father would not permit it. I was to follow him into the rabbinate—and become, like him, a great Talmudic scholar. My mother, Nechama (*z"l*)—a name that means "comfort" or "redemption" in Hebrew—was indeed my comfort growing up. As a child, you knew your grandmother for only a few years before she died, but she was a kind and broad-minded woman. She bought me a violin when I was seven, and it was love at first sight! But while my father liked music, he was suspicious about anything that might take me away from my Jewish studies—and so, he discouraged me from practicing and gave me dirty looks when I played my beloved violin for my own enjoyment.

And so, a rabbi I became. But my faith was always shaky, and my scholarship, even shakier. Can you imagine what it was like for me, a congregational rabbi, to speak to our families about the *Shoah*? Many of them had lost family members to Mr. Hitler, of course. Some had numbers from Auschwitz tattooed on their arms. And you may remember, Adam, we lost my dear cousin Shmuel to the ovens. I had to stand behind the *bimah* and tell my congregants that we, as mere humans, could never presume to understand G-d's point of view—that His knowledge is so radically different from our own that we are not even able to express this in language. You see, I was making the same argument Rambam made in the *Guide*—I mean, in his analysis of Job. You may recall—and please forgive me one last lesson, Adam!—Maimonides' comment on poor old Job: that the man's big mistake was ". . . . imagining [G-d's] knowledge to be similar to ours . . . [and] His intention, providence, and rule similar to ours." (ch. XXIV, *Guide of the Perplexed*). In other words, for Rambam, Job was something of a shmoe—and we'd be shmoes, too, I told my congregation, if we second guessed G-d about the Holocaust! I don't think our congregation ever bought it, and I wasn't really convinced myself.

And yet, Adam, I hounded you on all matters Jewish, from the time you refused to go to Hebrew school, to your rebellion against becoming *bar mitzvah*—a "son of the commandment"—to your decision to go to Cornell, instead of to Yeshiva. It must have felt like I had my hands around your throat, all those years! And all those rituals, prayers, injunctions, ceremonies, *mitzvot*, prohibitions—what does it all mean, anyway? Do we need such trappings to be decent human beings? After all, nowhere in the Talmud are we commanded to be "good Jews"—only good human beings! In my later years, I have come around to the sentiment expressed so well by our sage, Rabbi Abraham Joshua Heschel: "When I was young I admired clever people. Now that I am old, I admire kind people."

But my shame goes deeper than my masquerading as a holy man, Adam. I can recall, when you were a teenager—in junior high school, I believe—I used to make fun of your long, shaggy hair. I called it "effeminate." I think I even muttered to your mother once—and maybe you overheard this?—the word *"faygeleh"*. Such an ugly word, yet—may G-d forgive me!—I may have used it! Adam, if you overheard that slur, I beg you to forgive me—and I hope that if *you* forgive me, Hashem will, too.

What is most shameful is that I, of all people, should have known better. You see, when I was an adolescent, I was quite thin and frail, I also suffered with asthma—and my voice was nasal and high-pitched. Now, at that time, my family was living on the Lower East Side of New York, and I was being schooled at the Downtown Talmud Torah, at 394 East Houston Street. This was the early 1950s, remember, and the whole topic of homosexuality was of course taboo, especially among the Orthodox. Anyway, there was an older boy at this school—I can still see that smirking face of his—who once came up behind me, yanked off my yarmulke, and spoke that terrible word into my ear: *faygeleh!* I felt too ashamed to tell anyone, Adam! I picked up my yarmulke and ran home, fighting back tears. I wouldn't talk about it with my father or mother, but I never forgot the incident. And yet,

I made you feel ashamed of your long, shaggy hair, when you were just being a normal teen-age boy! I wonder how often we hound our children for the flaws or failings we see in ourselves—or persecute them for traits within ourselves that we refuse to face. I pray, Adam, that you will forgive me for this, and also that you never inflict such pain upon your own children, should you be blessed enough to have any. By the way, your Cornell girlfriend, Rebecca—she seems very nice, and is also very pretty! And I know that her father, Prof. Kornbluth, is considered a great scholar in his own field. I'm glad I got to meet her, if only briefly, on two occasions, and I hope she proves worthy of you. Who knows? Maybe someday she'll make you a good wife! I regret that I will not be around to see how your life story turns out, Adam. No doubt, you will make something of yourself—in the field of literature, or in whatever endeavor you pursue. And, of course, I hope you will take good care of your mother—after all, as they say, you will soon be the *balebos*—"the man of the house!" And please know, Adam, that for all the *tsuris* I brought down on your young head, I have always been proud of you—and I have always loved you.

With all my heart (*lev!*),
Your father

Chapter 23

What, is the Old King Dead?

The night before Professor Elie Kornbluth died, apparently of a pulmonary embolism, his daughter had visited him in his bedroom.

"What, Rivkaleh, no art work for me today?" the old man had said, smiling, and sitting up in bed.

"Not today, *Tateh*!" Rebecca reverted to the Yiddish for "Daddy", unsure of whether her father truly perceived her as a little girl, bringing home her water colors from school, or whether he was simply being playful.

"You always wanted to be an artist, and you have so much talent! You shouldn't let go of that dream, darling. What is it you do nowadays, anyway?"

"I'm a lawyer now, Dad." Rebecca had bitten down on her lip to keep from crying.

"Oh, yes, of course. But that sounds dreadfully dull, Rivkeleh! You should go back to painting. Such lovely water colors, you used to bring me!"

Elie Kornbluth had left no indication of what sort of memorial service he wanted, or even where he wanted to be buried. His will, such as it was, had been made out ten years ago, before his illness, and simply specified how his estate would be distributed—with virtually all of the money going to Adam, Rebecca, and Joel. Elie Kornbluth had never been "Jewishly observant", as popular parlance would have it; in fact, the man had been famously agnostic all his life, and had never gone to the synagogue during his adulthood, even on the high holidays. So the idea of holding a traditional Jewish burial ceremony, with a rabbi presiding, seemed odd and a bit perverse to Rebecca.

Her mother was buried in New Haven, where Elie still had several colleagues from his Yale days. But the thought of flying her father's body to New Haven, where very few of her own friends could attend a memorial service, gave Rebecca pause—maybe it would be better to bury her father here, in Hope Falls, where it would be far easier to visit his grave? But then, the idea of separating her father from her mother, even in death, bothered Rebecca, and she wondered if she was favoring the Hope Falls burial simply to make things easier on herself. *Then again*, she thought, *what's so bad about that, after one's father dies?* With that, she allowed herself a minute or two of quiet sobbing, then pulled herself together and put up a pot of coffee.

She and Adam conferred on the matter, and in the end, decided on a Hope Falls burial in two days. There was a non-denominational cemetery only five miles from the house, and several Hope Falls faculty were buried there—so, in a manner of speaking, Elie would rest among colleagues. The cemetery overlooked a lovely, rolling meadow, dotted with apple trees, and this thought somehow comforted Rebecca. Of course, she would telephone as many of Elie's Yale colleagues as she could locate, to inform them of the burial and invite them to say a few words at the graveside. Adam agreed to place an immediate death notice in the Hope Falls Sentinel, giving the time and place of the burial service, and would alert the drama department faculty at the college, most of whom were well-acquainted with Elie Kornbluth's seminal works on Shakespeare. (The risk of Ivor Somerset's showing up did cross Levtov's mind, but there was little to do about that very irritating possibility).

Their decision seemed abundantly validated when they told Marisol of the plan, and, of course, invited her to join the family at the graveside. Marisol—who had attended to all of Elie's needs these past few years, and who had discovered him dead in his bedroom—broke down in tears of gratitude. "*Ay, Gracias a Dios!* I thank you, Señora Rebecca!" she had cried, squeezing Rebecca's hand.

* * *

Chapter 24

You Shall Find Me a Grave Man

As Rebecca, Adam and Joel drove to the cemetery, Rebecca felt a sudden wave of shame wash over her. She was about to bury the man who had raised her nearly on his own, after burying his beloved wife—the man who had sung Elizabethan lullabies to her when she was too frightened to go to sleep. *Balow, my Babe, lie still and sleep, It grieves me sore to hear thee weep.* She had expected the end of her father's life to leave her awash in deep, unalloyed grief. Yet what Rebecca felt most strongly was relief. The aching burden of caring for her demented father had finally been lifted. No more calls from the police, as they chased Elie off the neighbors' property! No more sleepless nights, listening to the old man crooning Yiddish songs at the top of his lungs! No more of his damnable pissing in the sink! The sense of responsibility that had felt like an iron band around Rebecca's chest at last had slipped off. Finally, she could breathe fully and freely—except, of course, for the tightening knot of her guilt.

And there was another unsettling complication to ponder: now that Rebecca's time and energy would no longer be drained by an ailing father, would Adam press even more fervently for having another child? Or would he be too caught up in the scandal of his plagiarism to take that tack? Rebecca shook her head as if to dislodge these ruminations from her brain, prompting quizzical looks from Adam and Joel. "I'm OK," she said, preemptively, "I'm just a little tired."

Marisol had chosen to drive her own car to the cemetery—a beat-up, 2000 Ford Fiesta—and trailed close behind the family. The four of them were the first to arrive at the cemetery, which still lay under a good six inches of snow—the crusted remnants of the mid-December blizzard. The grave had already been dug out of the frozen ground, and a neat, pyramidal pile of dirt sat nearby. The cemetery caretaker soon emerged from a small stone building, rubbing his hands and stomping his feet uncomfortably. He was a tall, rail-thin man who looked to be in his seventies, and who struck Levtov as a man not far from the clutch of cold earth, himself. The man introduced himself simply as "Baxter," tersely explained the burial process, and—without awaiting any questions from the family—began to manipulate a large, stainless-steel frame that straddled the empty grave. This, Levtov assumed, was the device that would lower Elie's casket into its final resting place. As the old caretaker turned a metal crank that appeared to tighten two nylon straps, he began to hum a tune that Levtov vaguely associated with an old Doris Day movie—was it, "Tea for Two"? Adam and Rebecca exchanged looks of disbelief, and Adam could not resist whispering to his wife the line from Hamlet: *"Has this fellow no feeling of his business, that he sings at grave-making?"*

Rebecca and Adam, by this time, were growing increasingly nervous. It was ten minutes before the appointed hour, and nobody but the family, Marisol, and the old caretaker was present. The hearse carrying Elie Kornbluth's body was supposed to have arrived by now—as were some of Elie's colleagues from New Haven. Rebecca had voiced some concerns regarding the local funeral home—it had garnered only 3 of 5 "stars" on an internet website called, "Eternallyyours.com"—but it was too convenient to pass up. Notwithstanding her father's agnosticism, Rebecca had chosen a plain pine box as his coffin, as Jewish law and tradition require. But save for the torn black ribbons pinned to their clothing—a symbolic rending of the mourners' garments—the Levtovs made no special gestures toward a "Jewish" burial ceremony. And Rebecca couldn't help smiling at her Goth son's appearance: Joel had reluctantly worn his one dark suit—a grudging concession to the "Abercrombies"—but, in lieu of a standard shirt and tie, had adorned himself in a black satin "pirate shirt," with a large ruffled collar and flared cuffs. When Adam gave his son a disapproving look earlier that morning, Joel had said simply, "Zayde would understand."

All at once, three vehicles pulled into the snow-crusted driveway adjacent to the grave site: the hearse from the 3-star funeral home, and two slightly battered SUVs with Connecticut plates. It seemed Elie's Yale colleagues had not deserted him after all, and Rebecca squeezed Adam's hand with tears in her eyes. The result of the triple incursion, however, was a kind of controlled chaos, as Adam conferred with two men from Sloan's Funeral Home, and Rebecca greeted ten of Elie's colleagues, as they extricated themselves from their shoulder belts and stepped carefully out of the SUVs. She recognized only one of the elderly scholars—a man she had known as "Uncle Zvi", during her childhood.

He was, in the highfalutin parlance of academe, Professor Emeritus Zvi Meier Kirshenbaum, one of Elie's closest friends and occasional co-authors—a scholar of great erudition, who held positions in both the Religious Studies and Comparative Literature Departments at Yale. Now in his late 70s, but looking quite hale, Kirshenbaum greeted Rebecca with open arms, and an expression composed equally of recognition, sorrow, and happiness. "*Rivkaleh!*" he said softly, hugging Rebecca to his chest. "It has been so many, many years! And I am so sorry about my dear friend and your loving father." Rebecca returned the warmth of the old man's greeting, and asked him if he would be so good as to say a few words in memory of Elie.

"It would be my great honor and privilege, Rebecca, if you don't mind my ad libbing it," he replied, with a twinkle in his eye. Rebecca now recalled that "Uncle Zvi" always had a wry and somewhat mischievous sense of humor, which had endeared him greatly to her father.

Meanwhile, the two men from the funeral home had concluded their discussion with Adam, and were now introducing themselves to the taciturn caretaker, evidently conferring on their respective graveside duties. The caretaker nodded intermittently, in glum agreement with the two well-dressed men from Sloan's. Suddenly, another car pulled up alongside the SUVs—a dark-blue BMW that Adam thought he recognized from the college. Of course, the department had been notified of the last-minute burial arrangements, but Levtov had not expected anyone from the college to show up. Yet now, emerging from the driver's side, wearing a dubiously mournful expression, was Professor Ivor Somerset. His passenger was the Chairman of the Department, Creighton Fitchley.

Somerset—dressed in a perfectly tailored, grey Cashmere topcoat—strode quickly over to Adam and Rebecca, first shaking Adam's hand, and murmuring, "Sorry, old fellow—Kornbluth was a tremendous scholar." Somerset then faced Rebecca, drew her close and—to Levtov's astonishment—planted a kiss so near Rebecca's mouth that she actually blushed, in stunned silence. "Oh, my dear Rebecca,"

Somerset said in a kind of stage whisper, "I'm so sorry. Your father was truly a great man!" Levtov had the fleeting fantasy of grabbing one of the shovels near Elie's gravesite and smashing Somerset's skull into subatomic particles. In fact, he did nothing, save for nodding stiffly in The Serpent's direction. In his seething state, Levtov barely registered the condolences offered by Creighton Fitchley, who knew Elie's work intimately.

One of the men from the funeral home asked for six "volunteers" to serve as pallbearers, and after a brief discussion, six of Elie's younger colleagues haltingly carried the pine coffin from the hearse to the grave site and placed it in atop the lowering device. Rebecca then called upon Zvi Kirshenbaum to say a few words. Struggling to keep his fedora from blowing off in the brisk, early January wind, Uncle Zvi paused to search the faces of the gathered mourners. He spoke in a raspy but resonant voice.

"Those of you who knew Elie Kornbluth only as a superb scholar—a kind of prophet, in fact, in Shakespearean studies—missed out on the wonderful opportunity I enjoyed: knowing Elie as a friend and confidant. I first met Elie when we were both junior faculty at Yale—long before some of my younger colleagues here today were out of graduate school! I had the pleasure of being taken into the Kornbluth home, almost like a family member, and Elie's lovely daughter, Rebecca—Rivkaleh—was as close to my heart as my own flesh and blood. Now, you are all aware of Elie Kornbluth's magisterial works on Shakespeare—works that revolutionized our way of thinking about the Bard—but few of you knew the courage Elie showed during some of the darkest days of our republic. So, I take you back to 1968, when our country was riven with protests over the expanding war in Vietnam. Those of you of a certain age will recall that in January of that year, our own Yale chaplain, William Sloan Coffin, had been indicted on charges of conspiracy—conspiracy to encourage dodging the draft! Along with Spock and Raskin and Goodman, Bill Coffin—hmm, I can almost hear Elie chuckling over the unconscious significance of "Coffin" on a day like today!—well, anyway, Bill Coffin was indicted by a federal grand jury, you see. "Conspiracy to counsel, aid and abet draft resistance", if I am not mistaken, was the precise charge. Now, what does all this have to do with our dear, departed friend, Elie Kornbluth? Well, you see, Bill Coffin had riled up the administrators and bureaucrats at Yale. He had called for declaring Battell Chapel at Yale a sanctuary for draft resisters. I had joined with him in this call, and the big, gray suits in the Yale administration didn't like that. There I was, a young assistant professor in the Divinity School, making common cause with this firebrand, this indicted conspirator! And all this, at a time when I was up for promotion to Associate Professor. So, one day, I was called to the office of the Dean of the Divinity School—a very decent and scholarly man, to be sure, but one also aware of the political pressures of the administration. He urged me to "carefully consider" the anti-war stance I was taking, and how it might affect the school's reputation—and my future prospects at Yale. I was a little shook up, I'll tell you! A week later, I received a letter from the Vice Provost of the whole damn university—warning me about my "conspiring" with Bill Coffin, and how this might damage my chances for promotion. Well, enter my friend, Elie Kornbluth. Like me, Elie was a lowly assistant professor, but already, he had gained national attention for some of his work on Shakespeare's sonnets—and he had a stellar reputation as a man of honor and integrity. Now, Elie was in sympathy with the anti-war movement, but he was too wrapped up in his scholarly work to get directly involved. But when I showed him the letter from the Vice Provost, he blew up! I mean, he threw the damn letter into the garbage and started fuming about "the damn fascists"! The next day, Elie actually accompanied me to the Vice Provost's office—I think his name was Eilers or Eilman—and spoke in my behalf. He warned this Eilers fellow that the entire reputation of Yale University would be tarnished, if the administration were exposed as harassing and intimidating its own faculty. Elie Kornbluth was so eloquent—in that deep, baritone voice of his—that the Vice Provost actually apologized to me, right there in his office! And then, to top it all off . . . ."

By the time Uncle Zvi had concluded his rather lengthy comments, his nose had turned a bright red, the mourners were stomping and shivering, and Levtov's stomach was growling miserably. Levtov had planned to say a few words in memory of his father in law, but decided to forego the opportunity and allow his son to speak. After all, nobody present—not even Rebecca—had been as close to Elie Kornbluth in his final weeks as Joel Levtov.

The boy stepped up beside the grave, tugging his ruffled collar tight around his neck. He had worn a wool top coat over his suit, but still shivered in the brisk January breeze, which unsettled his dark, blond-streaked curls.

"Zayde—he was my friend," the boy began. "I guess, maybe, he was a better friend than some of the kids I used to hang out with. At least Zayde was honest and not, like, a double-crosser and stuff." Joel shifted uneasily and seemed to fight for control of his feelings. "When I would go into Zayde's bedroom, it was, like, you were transported back to another time—when people accepted you for what you are. OK, so, maybe it wasn't really like that in Elizabethan times—I guess there was a lot of prejudice against the Jews, and I know, like, even Shakespeare had some of that, at least when it came to Shylock. But Zayde never judged me. He always gave me the feeling that if I was true to myself—you know, "To thine own self be true"—everything would turn out OK. So, even our cat, Pupik, who likes to scratch you for no reason, even she would calm down in Zayde's room. And I guess I'm really gonna miss him." At that point, Joel directed his gaze toward the gravesite, and, with breaking voice, said, "I love you, Zayde."

By this time, the mourners were ready for warmth and nourishment—not more speeches. As they gathered around the grave, the old caretaker released the braking mechanism on the lowering device, and the straps that supported Elie Kornbluth's coffin slowly unwound, allowing the pine box to settle into the grave. Each of the mourners took turns shoveling a little soil atop the coffin—a Jewish custom Rebecca had requested, at the last minute. Levtov was not certain, but he thought the caretaker was still humming "Tea for Two", as the Great Man's coffin was slowly covered with dirt.

*   *   *

Chapter 25

Lunch at the St. Lawrence Grill

Levtov had taken a Friday afternoon off, indulging in one of his deepest and most sensual pleasures: eating at the St. Lawrence Grill. A week after Elie Kornbluth's funeral, the Levtov household was still in a period of adjustment and transition. There was no "sitting shiva" in the religious sense, but a few of Rebecca's close friends had stopped by to comfort and commiserate, laden with coffee cake, stuffed cabbage, and bowls of soup. Rebecca was busy dealing with Elie's estate, which, to everyone's surprise, was in excess of a million dollars. Apparently, for all his scholarly immersion in the 16th century, the Great Man had shown considerable skill with 21st century investment strategies. Rebecca had taken the day off, too, and was home gathering together Elie's clothing, scholarly papers, and his collection of Elizabethan instruments—including a well-preserved lute said to have been in the possession of The Virgin Queen herself. Marisol, meanwhile, had been retained to assist in general household chores and was now busy boxing up Elie's library of some three thousand volumes. Adam and Rebecca had decided to donate half the books to Yale University, and half to the very modest Hope Falls College library.

Levtov had frequented the St. Lawrence Grill for nearly the entire twenty years he had taught at the college. He loved the food—mostly soul-satisfying dishes, like shepherd's pie, lasagna, pastrami and brisket—but he enjoyed the ambience even more. Upon first entering the large, walnut-paneled restaurant, the customer was greeted by an old-fashioned lunch counter, complete with red leather swivel-stools and a wooden counter top. This was the preferred seating area for the younger crowd, including many college students, as it facilitated both casual conversation and the more concerted "pick-up." To the left of the counter was a general seating area of tables and booths, surrounded by seven-foot high, mahogany bookcases. These were filled with the classics of philosophy, literature and religion—and therein lay the history of the St. Lawrence Grill, and Levtov's avid attraction to it.

Most people who didn't know the restaurant's story assumed that it was named for the St. Lawrence River, which ran about two hundred miles to the north of Hope Falls. But this was true only in a derivative sense. More than twenty-five years ago, a former Jesuit priest and Hope Falls College professor experienced what some colleagues had termed "a psychotic break." No doubt this was unfair, in as much as Prof. Colm Shaughnessy possessed quite as much sanity as the average Hope Falls College faculty member—for what that was worth—though tainted by a certain impetuousness that caused him many problems. In 1987, the young Fr. Shaughnessy was booted from the Jesuit order for what was called "insubordination." In truth, his expulsion was the result of his ministering to gay and lesbian Catholics, despite having been admonished to cease said activity, by then Cardinal Joseph Ratzinger—later to become Pope Benedict XVI. Shaughnessy himself was not gay, but he believed fervently in the need to bring gay and lesbian Catholics "into the bosom of Mother Church." Having been expelled from the Jesuits, he became, albeit briefly, a professor in the Religious Studies department of Hope Falls College, before undergoing what he himself described as a "crisis of faith." As Shaughnessy had put it in one of many conversations with Levtov, "I did not cease merely believing in God. I ceased to believe in God's *goodness*, given the manifest power and majesty of evil in the world." Shaughnessy resigned from the Hope Falls faculty after only a year, and decided that his real calling was as a "feeder of the poor and hungry." But the young apostate never abandoned his belief in the power of conscience or of personal integrity. He was, in fact, an ardent admirer of the third-century Christian martyr, St. Lawrence—who, by tradition and legend, was literally grilled to death by the Roman authorities.

"You see, Adam, my friend," Shaughnessy had once explained over a beer, "St. Lawrence had a cocky sense of humor, and for that, I greatly admire him. Legend has it that while being roasted alive on the gridiron, he quipped, "I'm well done on that side. Turn me over!" Well, of course, that's undoubtedly apocryphal, but you can see why dear St. Larry is the patron saint of cooks—and why I simply *had* to name my little restaurant, "The St. Lawrence Grill." And, of course, Larry is also patron saint of the poor—which is why there is always free soup available to anyone who comes to my place hungry."

Levtov sat alone in one of the booths, contemplating his own spiritual crisis, sustained by a heaping plate of brisket and a glass of Merlot. He knew that the reckoning was nearly upon him. Ignatieff had been clear: he, Adam Levtov, had to come clean in the matter of his plagiarism. But what would this mean, in practice? At a minimum, Levtov would need to confess his crime to Creighton Fitchley. But would this satisfy Ignatieff and his "legal advisor", the hulking Russian bear? Or would Ignatieff demand a more humiliating public confession?

Levtov was keenly aware of what was likely to happen to his academic career, after such a revelation: there was a "zero tolerance" policy at Hope Falls College, when it came to plagiarism. Eight years ago, Egon Von Scheuler, a much-admired, tenured professor in the History Department, had been found guilty of cribbing a few passages, in one of his books, from another scholar. The Dean of the college gave him a simple ultimatum: resign immediately or be fired. Von Scheuler had wound up, a month later, teaching English at a prep school somewhere in Argentina.

Naturally, the notion of being fired horrified Levtov—the mere thought of it now caused a wild fluttering beneath his sternum. And yet, he also found something oddly exhilarating in the prospect of dismissal. Levtov had been long aware that, for him, teaching was largely an honorable compromise. Teaching had allowed him to pursue his love of the theater while comfortably ensconced in the cloister of academe. And in that quasi-monastic setting, there were the quiet satisfactions of publication and promotion, conferences and conclaves—and the self-inflating puffery that led one to imagine he might inspire his students to a career in the theater. But Levotv knew that teaching also had served as a convenient excuse—even a plausible explanation—for abandoning playwriting, his abiding passion. And with that realization came the fear that he was now incapable of writing anything enduring and worthwhile—something that emerged from his own soul and not from the mind of Grigory Ignatieff.

Suddenly, Levtov's rumination was interrupted by a familiar voice. "Yo, Professa Liftoff!"

Levtov had not seen Jabari Frazier since the end of Fall Semester. Now, during "winter break", most of the students had left town, though the college library and residence halls remained open.

"Hey, Jabari!" Levtov was not certain why, but he felt genuinely happy to see the strapping young man who had carried off the role of Othello so convincingly—despite Levtov's early misdirection. Levtov stood up and shook his student's hand. "How have you been? I figured you'd be back home during break."

"Naw, I'm still in my dorm room, Professa. My folks, they in Syracuse, you know, but I got all my friends here. Plus, my dad—we don't always see eye to eye, you know what I'm sayin?"

"Oh, yes, I certainly do," Levtov said in a subdued voice. "I'm sure that's kinda rough on you, Jabari. Um—would you like to sit down and grab a coffee, or . . ."

Frazier smiled. "Thanks, Professa, but I gotta run. I just wanted to tell you, I really liked bein' in the play. I mean, I know we kinda butted heads fo' a while, but I think we came out OK. And, you know what, man? I'm thinkin' I'd like to learn how to direct, you know, like what you do, maybe more than acting."

"Wow, Jabari, that's terrific! I mean—it's hard work, directing, but very rewarding. I can put you in touch with some good people at S.U. They have a big drama department, and . . ."

"Syracuse University? You know what? A guy from S.U. saw our play and came up to me afterward to shake my hand. Alonzo . . . Alonzo Capa . . ."

"Alonso Caputi? No kidding? I didn't see him in the audience, but he is tremendous! He's directed some of the best productions in the state."

"Yeah, well, anyway, he say he liked what I did and to get in touch. You know, maybe take a seminar with him or somethin'."

Frazier wrapped up the conversation quickly and said a polite good-bye. Levtov poured himself some more Merlot and gulped it down, struggling with feelings of pride, dread and anticipatory humiliation. Had he actually inspired one of his students to become a director? Well, *mazel tov*—it was about damn time! But to sit in Creighton Fitchley's office and confess his crime; and then, to face Jabari Frazier in the hall, having been dismissed from his teaching position—all this was more than Levtov could stomach at once. That familiar translucency he had known for so long again began to inhabit him, thinning his bones and flesh from the inside. But this time, the sensation came with the knowledge that others would soon see through him in ways that would alter his life forever.

Chapter 26

In the Principal's Office

Rebecca had been dead-set against Adam's confessing. She had her lawyer's hackles up, and argued that, with a proper defense, her husband could fight the plagiarism charge. "Who's to say that you lifted that scene from Ignatieff?" she asked, spilling coffee from her mug as she gestured rhetorically, pacing around the living room. "How could they prove that, since the play was translated from Russian into English? And, honey, you said yourself that you "adapted" the material to suit your needs. You shouldn't admit anything until I have the guys at the firm take a look at the case. Think about your tenure, your position and . . ."

"Thanks, but I know what I did, Bec," Adam had interrupted, "Now it's time to own up."

Rebecca lodged a few more perfunctory protests, but soon abandoned the effort. She knew that her husband's corrosive sense of guilt would dissolve whatever rational arguments she could muster.

Creighton Fitchley was one of those decent, gentle, but unlucky men whose hormonal endowment simply never permitted his moustache to grow in with conviction. Sitting behind his desk, across from Levtov, Fitchley conjured up the image of a tweed-clad Teddy Bear, decked out in a dark-blue bow tie and squinting behind his horn rim glasses, which sat slightly askew. Fitchley was not a man well-disposed to making administrative decisions, much less those that required hard-nosed discipline or punishment. His first instinct, in any crisis, was to ask for "clarification of the relevant facts;" and, if necessary, to appoint an appropriate committee to study the matter. But Levtov feared that this time, Fitchley would have only one tenable option.

"Well, Adam, now then, now then—good to see you!" Fitchley drummed his fingers noisily on his desktop. "And kudos, once again, on the excellent *Othello*. I've heard very good things from many of the faculty. Oh, and, once again, my condolences on your father-in-law's passing. I was privileged to have attended the very moving graveside service. Well, so, you said you had something important to discuss with me?"

As Levtov prepared to disclose his crime, he was suddenly cast back to those days in elementary school, when a boy's misdeeds would compel a visit to the principal's office. It had happened to him only once in grade school, after he had made some snide remark about the lunch being served in the school cafeteria—was it the "fish sticks" they served on Fridays, in deference to the Catholic kids? And had he really referred to them as "*Pish* sticks"? The woman collecting lunch tokens had overheard young Adam's snotty comment, and promptly reported him to the principal, Mr. Klemp. The boy had received a stern lecture on "respect and good manners" from Klemp and had been sent home early. Far more humiliating, Adam's parents had been notified of their son's "outrageous" behavior. Rabbi Levtov had spent the next three days hammering the boy with Biblical and Talmudic maxims: *"Rise before the elderly and show honor before the aged"* (Leviticus 19:32); *"Parents bring a child into this world but a teacher can bring a child into the World to Come,"* and on and on. (Rabbi Levtov did not seem to grasp that the woman who had taken Adam's lunch token was a cafeteria employee, not a teacher, but the browbeaten boy had decided not to press the point). Suddenly, Levtov had a pang of sympathy for poor Joel, who, not long ago, had been called to the principal's office for the innocuous act of wearing black eyeliner to school.

"Adam?" Creighton Fitchley said, sounding puzzled. "Are you OK? You seem to be drifting off somewhere . . . ."

"I'm very sorry, sir—um, Creighton—I was just trying to figure out how to tell you what I need to tell you. This is really painful and, well—deeply embarrassing."

And so Levtov began his narration of the chain of events, going back to early 1998, when he had first started working on "Lustig the Tummler." He explained how he had discovered the translated manuscript of Grigory Ignatieff's play, "The Comic," in his late father-in-law's library. He explained how his own writing had gotten stuck—how he had panicked for weeks, until he realized that "Lustig" could be saved though the artful appropriation of the third act of Ignatieff's play. Finally, Levtov paused and let escape a deep, involuntary sigh. Though it seemed like years to him, only ten minutes had passed.

Creighton Fitchley, whose complexion had gradually blanched in the course of hearing Levtov's confession, looked as if someone had stuck a knitting needle into his cervical spinal cord.

"Um, Adam, I—I must confess . . . please forgive me if I am misunderstanding you, but—this "appropriation" of Ignatieff's material—are you saying . . . are you telling me that you *plagiarized* the third act of your play? The play we all felt so proud of, in the department? And so proud of *you*!

Surely, there must be some extenuating—I mean, I am just trying to clarify the relevant facts!"

Ah, dear Creighton! Levtov thought, with tears welling in his eyes—always the supreme clarifier. Always the one to await a more charitable and humane explanation. Always the one to seek some saving grace in the blundering or malfeasance of others. A dangerous habit of mind, some cynics might claim, finding in Fitchley the sort of person who might hear the genocidal plans of an Eichmann or a Hitler, and ask ever-so-politely for a "clarification of the relevant facts." But in these circumstances, Levtov was hardly in a position to sit in judgment.

The meeting went on for another twenty minutes. During that interval, as Levtov grew more animated—elaborating with considerable energy on his meeting with Grigory Ignatieff—Creighton Fitchley grew increasingly quiet. His face had taken on the expression one often sees in taxidermy specimens: a gently mortified fixity that is neither of the living, nor of the dead, but of the expertly gutted and stuffed. Finally, Fitchley adjusted the position of his glasses, cleared his throat and spoke. His voice was subdued and kindly.

"Well, um, of course, Adam, I'm quite sympathetic to your situation. You have been a valued faculty member here for over eighteen years. But, as you know, Hope Falls College has a very clear policy . . . that is to say, unless the relevant facts are somehow other than they seem, I have no real choice but, uh—I'm so sorry, Adam—to ask for your immediate resignation."

"Yes, sir," Levtov replied, in a voice he barely recognized—a voice so uncannily calm, it might have belonged to an elderly funeral director, reassuring a bereaved father that his son's service would be the very model of decorum. "Of course, sir. My actions have left you no choice. I'll submit my resignation immediately." Levtov was surprised to find himself overcome by a deep sense of relief. A faint smile crossed his face, much to Critchley's puzzlement.

There was an extended discussion of how the resignation would work: how the formal letter of resignation should be written; how Levtov's final pay check for services rendered would be handled; and how the unfortunate event would be announced in the departmental bulletin. There was further discussion of how Levtov's classes could be taken over by others on the faculty; but by this time, Levtov had drifted into a kind of reverie, in which Critchley's voice had become a vague, burbling murmur. Levtov recalled, some hours later, shaking Critchley's hand and muttering something about "a great privilege" and "so very sorry"—but the final minutes of their meeting seemed to have leaked out of Levtov's brain.

It was well past five o'clock, and already dark outside. Even the redoubtable Gwen Wallace had left for the day. Levtov, his mind wrapped in a kind of anodyne gauze, shambled his way from Critchley's office to his own. He gazed around the tiny, overheated room and heaved a sigh. There was the familiar "Mr. Coffee" machine that had served him faithfully since 1998. There were the overloaded shelves of his treasured books, badly in need of dusting; and the piles of manila folders, filled with the moldering drafts of unpublished articles. How little he had completed, after all these years: a flyspeck, really, on the wall of his vaunted ambitions. And on the shelf above his desk, Levtov scanned, for the last time, the reassuring plaques and knick-knacks that give academics the illusion their efforts matter in the wider world: a much-prized "Teacher of the Year" award from 1999, one year after "Lustig" had premiered; a photo of a smiling Levtov shaking hands with the Mayor of Syracuse, upon the establishment of the Rod Serling Theater Arts Scholarship, which had brought Jabari Frazier to the college; and a framed letter from Ben Brantley, congratulating Levtov on *"your very amusing play, 'Lustig the Tummler' . . ."*

He packed up two boxes of books and papers, along with the battle-worn Mr. Coffee, and headed out to the parking lot. By this time, Levtov's mood of numb despair had given way to an unexpected and paradoxical elation. True, his academic career was over—as the cliché would have it, "ended in disgrace." And yet, strangely, Levtov felt as if he were gazing down upon his life from an exhilarating height, like the vista ten-year old Adam had taken in from the Ferris wheel at the Genesee County Fair. A breathless expectancy filled him now, as if anything were possible, if only he could summon sufficient will.

But once in the college parking lot, Levtov's euphoria was instantly checked. Standing one row down from his car was the insufferable Somerset, fumbling in the dark with his keys.

"Ah, Adam, dear boy!" came the slurred and plummy voice, "Good to see you! Homeward bound after a long day, are we?" The Englishman, obviously drunk, wobbled slightly and braced himself against the door of his car.

"Yes, a long day, Somerset," Levtov said with unaccustomed vigor, "and a long time enduring your smarmy jollity and Oxbridge anti-Semitism!"

Somerset looked stricken. "Are you off your bloody trolley, dear boy? Have you been drink . . . *urp* . . . drinking?"

"I am quite on my trolley, which will take me far from the likes of you, Somerset. And by the way, keep your goddamn hands off Rebecca, in the unlucky event we run into you somewhere!"

Somerset's lip curled into the snarl of a junk-yard dog. "What . . . what in blazes are you talking about, you knackered little poof! Just because you can't keep your wife satisfied in bed, don't go accusing me of . . ."

"I saw the little message you wrote to Rebecca, Somerset—that "hanky-panky" note you slipped into her briefcase!"

But at this, Somerset's face registered blank bafflement. "Note? What note? You are completely barmy, my dear fellow, and I suggest you exit the stage before you fall through the fucking trap door!"

Having been freed from the usual social expectations of his job, and still feeling giddily hypomanic, Levtov was more than ready for a little theatricality. As he slid into his car seat, he let fly his farewell to Somerset.

"And I suggest, Ivor, that you well and truly sod off!"

* * *

Chapter 28

When, in disgrace with fortune and men's eyes . . .

The first week was the hardest. Among the faculty of the small college, word had spread quickly of Levtov's "resignation", which was widely viewed as an outright dismissal. A brief item in the department bulletin had noted that, "With deep regret, Prof. Fitchley has accepted the immediate resignation of Prof. Adam Levtov, owing to a violation, in 1998, of the college's policies regarding appropriate citation of published materials. This violation was disclosed fully and voluntarily by Prof. Levtov." This, Levtov felt, was as benign a condemnation of his crime as could have been phrased in English, without sounding frankly Orwellian. The local paper—*The Hope Falls Herald*—had run an ambiguous story regarding, "Professor Adam Levtov's sudden and unexplained resignation from the college," tartly noting that, "Repeated attempts to clarify the circumstances of Levtov's departure have not been successful." Translation: Creighton Fitchley was not dropping a dime on his long-time colleague and protégé.

Levtov could not bring himself to show his face at the college during regular hours and had taken to clearing out the remaining items in his office well after six p.m. Each time he walked down the corridor carrying boxes of books and papers, he said a silent prayer that he would not run into Jabari Frazier. The very idea of meeting his student's gaze was too painful to contemplate. Fortunately, it was still winter break, and only a few students and faculty had occasion to visit the department. Jabari Frazier, thankfully, was not among them.

For the first few days after Adam's resignation, the Levtov household was eerily quiet. With Elie now gone and Marisol's visits nearly eliminated, the accustomed noises of the house had been muted. It came as a surprise to both Adam and Rebecca that Elie's manic howling and crooning were so sorely missed. "Oh, God, what I would give," Rebecca said wistfully, "to hear Pop singing, *"Belz, my little town of Belz!"* at the top of his lungs, just one more time!" And Joel, who had been so close to his Zayde in those final days, seemed disinclined to blast the house with the cacophony of Siouxsie and the Banshees, preferring, instead, to strum moody folk melodies on his new acoustic guitar. He and Seth Greenberg had been in frequent contact recently—even meeting for coffee at the St. Lawrence Grill—and their relationship seemed to have entered a delicate phase of rapprochement.

At dinner, the general dampening of the domestic atmosphere was magnified by the reticence of Rebecca and Joel, who were still trying to gauge Adam's emotional state. Levtov, of course, had informed his wife and son of his resignation. He had half-hoped that this would be followed by some expression of either anger ("Jesus, Adam, how could you fuck up your career and our lives like this?! What were you thinking?") or pity ("Don't take it so hard, Dad/Honey, we all make mistakes!"). But neither Rebecca nor Joel would raise the subject of Adam's resignation, and dinner was enveloped in a dense and discomfiting silence—a harsher punishment for Levtov, surely, than any expression of anger. Rebecca's eyes rarely met her husband's, over the dinner table, as she sullenly cut her brisket into increasingly small morsels.

Finally, on a night when Joel had gone off to a concert with Seth, Rebecca sat Adam down in the living room, poured them both a glass of Pinot Grigio, and placed her hand on his.

"You know what, hon? It's not the end of the world. OK, I'll admit it—I was pissed off when you resigned. I mean, it didn't feel like you had really thought it through. I was ready to fight the damn thing, you know. And I felt like you had sort of closed me out of the whole deal. But after I thought about it, I decided—well, I guess this was just something you had to do. Maybe it was your way of keeping faith with something or someone. I'm not really sure I understand it all. But, truth be told, we can live without your faculty salary. And, well—not to sound crass, but Pop's estate will definitely cushion the blow."

Adam smiled forlornly, and brushed aside a stray lock of hair on Rebecca's forehead. "Thanks, Bec. It's good to hear you say that. But, truth be told, I still feel like a hundred and sixty pounds of cow flop."

"Look, honey, you screwed up, I get it. But you also *owned* up. What's done is done. Now you have the rest of your life in front of you. And we have *our* lives, too. So let's figure out what we want to do with them!"

Levtov suddenly felt a twinge of anxiety. There was, of course, the volatile matter of their having another child. But somehow, and for reasons he did not quite fathom, Levtov felt the energy seeping slowly out of this heretofore overheated issue. His mind had turned, rather, to Ivor Somerset and the recent rancorous encounter in the parking lot. Since then,

Levtov had been ruminating on the apparent perplexity Somerset had shown when the matter of the "hanky-panky" note had been raised. Given the man's obvious inebriation, Levtov was inclined to give some credence to Somerset's claim of ignorance—following the adage, "*In vino veritas.*" (No less an authority than Elie Kornbluth was fond of noting that the Germanic tribes of classical times always drank when holding councils, as they believed no one could lie convincingly while drunk). But—if Somerset had not placed the "hanky-panky" note in Rebecca's attaché those many weeks ago, then how had it gotten there? For that matter, who had written it, complete with the "Ives" signature on college stationery? With considerable ambivalence, Levtov decided to broach the question with Rebecca.

"Yeah, um, Bec—before we get into the rest of our lives, can I ask—I mean, there's something from a few months ago that has been puzzling me. Nothing huge, just a pebble in the shoe sort of feeling."

Rebecca looked blankly at her husband. "Yeah, hon, go for it!" she said with a bit of forced cheer.

"OK, so—back in, I think, September, I was walking by your desk one night, and your attaché case was open. I happened to look down and I saw this—this note on college stationery, and it seemed to be from Ivor. It was actually signed, "Ives", and it was about some kind of dinner get-together. Oh, and—there was this weird allusion to, um, "hanky-panky." Does any of that ring a bell?"

Rebecca's face first grew very pale. She slapped her wine glass down on the coffee table with such force that the base cracked. Her eyes widened, and her cheeks flushed a deep crimson.

"Oh, God!" she said, her mouth drawn down at the corners. "Oh, Adam, this is really hard to talk about! What I did—it's so humiliating to have to . . . I mean . . . . oh, Jesus!" She fought back tears with all the lawyerly fortitude she could muster.

Adam put his hand on his wife's shoulder. "Hey, Bec, c'mon! After my gigantic, life-altering, not-to-mention-illegal fuck-up, how bad can it be? What? Were you and Ivor gonna run off to Tahiti?" He laughed miserably at his own question, praying that Rebecca's answer would not open some new can of soul-eating worms.

"Oh, God, honey—that damn note!—it was just after the faculty dinner, last summer. Remember? Everybody was a little tipsy, you know, and Ivor—I was on the couch with him . . ."

"Yeah, I remember it very clearly, Bec," Adam said with barely concealed irritation.

"OK, look—I know this is a sore point, hon. The thing is, Ivor had his hand on my knee, and you came by—oh, this sounds so stupid, Adam!—but anyway, here is this boozed-up Brit with his hand on my knee, and all you could say was, *"How do you guys like the shrimp?"* I was *so* pissed off at you! I mean, Jesus, you could have said *something* to fucking Ivor, and . . . ."

"It's OK, Bec. You were right to be pissed off. I should have said something to him. Actually, I should have punched out that smug, chiseled face of his, then and there, but instead . . ."

At this, Levtov had to fight back tears.

"What is it, hon? Instead what?"

"Instead I was kind of a chicken-shit, and I hated myself for it, Bec!"

At this, Rebecca put her hands on Adam's shoulder and pulled him close. "And I hated myself for writing that damn note and signing it "Ives"! I am so sorry, honey! I was furious

165

with you—I mean, that you just let that sleaze-ball paw me like that! And, well, obviously—cliché, cliché!—I was trying to make you jealous, and I'm really, really sorry!"

"It's OK, Bec. It's a relief to get this all out in the open. I guess it all makes me feel a little less like a stupid shit for all my screw-ups. And I'm sorry for hectoring you, all these months, about having another kid. You know, it's strange—the whole idea just doesn't seem all that important to me anymore, though I'm not sure why."

"Well, we can figure that out later, hon. Meanwhile, speaking of kids, Joel is out at that concert for the night." Rebecca's voice suddenly took on a theatrically husky and conspiratorial tone, as she leaned toward Adam's face. "Maybe we should, um, you know—*take advantage* of the empty house?"

Their lovemaking was fumbling and uncertain, like a couple wandering dazed through a neighborhood they once had known intimately. Adam felt himself trembling, and briefly experienced that sick, sinking feeling that men dread in the depths of their bones—the carnal equivalent of the stand-up comedian's "flop sweat." But the feeling passed as he held Rebecca in his arms. In the candle-lit bedroom, she was still the gorgeous co-ed Adam had kissed in the stacks of Uris Library, almost a quarter-century ago; only now, Rebecca's eyes betrayed a shy hesitancy that mirrored his own trepidation. Anger, fear, hope and love, all entangled, surged wildly through them, slowly giving way to arousal and comingling. And the ghostly transparency that had haunted Adam Levtov for fifteen years made no visitation.

Chapter 29

At Last, Back to the Sea

Finally: the end to what had seemed an endless winter. The last snow had fallen in late April, burying the pink crocuses for two days, but melting quickly in the rising heat of early May. In their yard, daffodils and forsythia now bloomed, and in the gardens of Hope Falls College, flox, columbine, and bleeding heart had sprung suddenly to life. Rebecca, though not an avid gardener, found special pleasure in a dense colony of yellow trout-lilies, nodding at the end of their slender stalks, only a few feet from their front door.

It was a bright Saturday afternoon, and the Levtovs had packed a picnic lunch for their drive into the country. Only a few miles south of Hope Falls, the landscape spread out in a carpet of vivid greens and pink apple blossoms, amidst rolling hills and red farm houses. "Share the Road" signs appeared at regular intervals, signaling drivers to watch out for the horse-drawn buggies of the newly-settled Amish. From the front passenger seat, Adam cast nervous glances at Joel, who was now driving with his recently-earned learner's permit. Rebecca sat in back, trying to suppress her cautionary kibitzing, while silently assessing her son's transformation over the past few months.

In just the last half-year, Joel had shot up at least two inches, and the croaking, breaking voice of early puberty had deepened into a reasonably solid baritone. The young man had largely abandoned the grungy, Goth wardrobe of the previous year, but the gold earring had been retained, and the blond streak still stood out against his coal-black curls. Dressed now in blue jeans, a light denim jacket, and a "*Hope Falls On its Ass*" tee shirt, Joel looked very much the "regular teenage guy," in Rebecca's assessment. He and Seth Greenberg were now, more or less officially, a couple; and Joel was comfortable referring to Seth as "my boyfriend", when discussing such matters with the family. The two had been teased a few times at school, where they were discreet about their relationship, but there had been no more offensive videos or sustained harassment. Along with his maturing voice and burgeoning height, Joel had "bulked up" impressively—the result of his recent weight-lifting regimen. Rebecca supposed, perhaps wishfully, that her son no longer presented such a tempting target for homophobic bullies.

Relations between Joel and his father were not ideal, but had improved in the past few months. Rebecca often wondered, now that Zayde was gone, if Joel felt the need to mend fences with his father; or, more optimistically, if Adam had grown more accepting of his son. After Joel acquired his learner's permit, he and Adam had taken to frequent drives in the country, and this ritual seemed to cement the bond that was developing between them. "I guess, with the driving, we sort of meet on common ground," Joel had commented to Rebecca, shrugging his shoulders. Not entirely to Rebecca's surprise, as Adam and Joel had become closer emotionally, her husband's lobbying for another child had subsided drastically. Perhaps the filial "do-over" no longer seemed necessary to Adam, who now seemed quietly accepting of his son.

Levtov had planned the trip to the Fiddler's Green Formation, near Ilion, New York, for nearly a week. Located about fifty miles to the east of Hope Falls, the formation represented one of the finest examples of Silurian period fossil preserves in the eastern U.S.—and was arguably the world's foremost site for eurypterid fossils.

"Eu-*what*erids?" Rebecca had asked dubiously, a few days ago.

"See, Honey," Adam had explained with the enthusiasm of his boyhood fossil-hunting days, "Eurypterids were sort of like sea scorpions! They were the fiercest predators of the sea, way back, oh, 400 million years ago. When I was a kid in Batavia, I used to look for trilobites, which are from roughly the same time period. The whole region was a huge, inland sea."

"Dad," Joel had chimed in, "I read that these guys—the eurypterids—they could grow to be, like, seven feet long!"

Against all expectations, Joel had taken an interest in Adam's boyhood passion of fossil hunting, even going so far as to take out some archaeology texts from the college library. Whether this represented a newfound way of getting closer to his father, or the fantasy of uncovering ancient mysteries, neither Adam nor Rebecca could say, but they were clearly pleased with their son's enthusiasm. And, in the past few months, Rebecca, too, had developed a new focus for her energies—or rather, she had rediscovered her own childhood passion for art. She was working just four days a week at the law firm now and using Fridays to develop a series of outdoor water colors, titled, "Hope Falls, A Town for All Seasons." (Old Man Malamud had muttered under his breath—something about "this rather dubious commitment to the firm"—but had not raised any objections to Rebecca's reduced schedule.)

A month after Levtov's resignation, Marisol—who now came in once weekly to do some light cleaning—had glimpsed a hulking figure approach the front door of the house, just as dusk was falling. The intruder had slipped something into the mailbox and quickly trotted off, evidently with no wish to be detected. That evening, Levtov anxiously examined the envelope, which bore the all too familiar, wild scrawl. His heart and temples pounding, he had torn open the envelope with trembling hands, fearing that his nemesis was about to deliver the *coup de grace*—perhaps in the form of a lawsuit. Instead, he found a photocopied article from *The Hope Falls Herald,* reporting on his resignation from the college, along with a note signed by Grigory Ignatieff. Unlike the playwright's usual hand-written missives, this one consisted of a single typed word, in Cyrillic script:

Подлинность

After a little online research, Levtov was able to transliterate the word as *"podlinnost"*—Russian for "authenticity." Pondering the meaning of this for the next few days, Levtov arrived at the view that the note was an oblique gesture of forgiveness on Ignatieff's part—or at least, a signal that no retribution would follow. Indeed, over the subsequent months, there were no further communications from the author of "The Comic."

In the interim, Levtov had enjoyed the liberation that sometimes accompanies dismissal and disgrace. Freed from all responsibilities save those of the small-town householder and family man—including, recently, ensuring that Pupik's food and water were replaced at appropriate intervals—Levtov had begun to write. The work was slow and sometimes painful—a bit like learning how to walk again, he imagined, after suffering a broken leg. But at least the words were coming: first, as snippets of dialogue, surfacing as he drifted off to sleep; and later, as full-blown scenes and characters. As each scene developed, Levtov's confidence grew. And, to his surprise and relief, the feeling of ghostly transparency had not returned.

He was not sure if the nascent play would veer toward the tragic or the comic; or whether it would fall into that ambiguous realm in which life and death mingle promiscuously and produce wild, chimerical offspring. Levtov was certain of only one thing: the title of the play would be, *The Director of Minor Tragedies*.

END

Afterword

While all the characters in this novel are fictional creations, some were inspired by actual persons and their experiences or views. The character and mannerisms of Elie Kornbluth, for example, was influenced by an interview with the great literary scholar, Harold Bloom, published in the *Paris Review* (Antonio Weiss was the interviewer). The character of Jabari Frazier was inspired by a story in the *Boston Globe*, concerning Antonio Stroud, a young African-American man from Roxbury, Mass., who was given the title role in a production of "Othello". I am indebted to Michael Forden Walker, Artistic Associate Interim Director of Youth Programs at the Actors' Shakespeare Project, for background information on how regional accents are handled in some productions of Shakespeare's plays. Thanks as well to Dr. Manuel Mota-Castillo for his help with some Spanish idioms. And, special thanks to Dr. Rich Berlin for his kind reading of the manuscript; and to Janice Eidus for her very helpful suggestions and comments on an earlier draft of the novel. The town of Hope Falls was entirely fictional, though there is a hamlet of Hope Falls in the Adirondacks region of New York State. References to Batavia, N.Y., where I was raised, are not intended as historically accurate statements, though they are loosely grounded in my early experiences there. The same may be said of the novel's descriptions of Cornell University, which I attended in the early 1970s.